I0631037

The Devil's Stronghold

Leslie Ford

The Devil's Stronghold

WILDSIDE PRESS

COPYRIGHT 1948
BY LESLIE FORD

The Devil's Stronghold

CHAPTER ONE

THE YELLOW MATCH BOOK was lying on the seat of the taxicab. I saw it as the doorman at Garfinckel's bowed me in with a punctilio worthy of the wife of the Combined Chiefs of Staff. "How you feelin', Miz Latham?" he asked. "How them two boys gettin' on these days?"

I recognized him then; it was the uniform that had blinded me. He was some kind of a cousin of my Lilac's, and a former neighbor in Georgetown. I was pleased to see him again.

"I'm fine, Boston, and the boys are too. Bill's out of the Navy and going to California Tech. You must come and see him when he gets home for Christmas. How are you?"

Boston was fine, and he'd certainly come and see Bill, who must have grown up considerable by now. He was so right—and at the moment I was so unaware of how right he was.

He held the taxi door open while I picked up the yellow matches. "It's a smutty day," he said. "That ol' cloud goin' to bust himself, any minute now."

He was right again. It was one of those poisonously hot late September days in Washington that usually end in a futile thunderstorm. I wouldn't, otherwise, have bothered to pick up the match book, but with everything else sticking to me I could do without a yellow stain on my white dress.

I gave the driver my address on P Street in Georgetown. It was then I saw what was scrawled on the match book as if someone had made a hurried note. "The Devil's Stronghold," it said. It seemed an astonishing notation. I suppose I could have thought of it as premonitory, some way, but experience has shattered all faith in my premonitions, and Hollywood to me was still only a fantastic other world I read about at hairdressers, or on the front page when its bizarre antics made it front page news. And I don't mean to imply that Hollywood is the Devil's Stronghold. Startled by that sinister note on the cover of the yellow match book, I automatically opened it. Inside was written, in the same hurried scrawl, "Death is the Devil's

3

Stronghold." Nothing more, nothing less . . . a simple statement of basic truth. And its only connection with any geographical place is that Hollywood, California, turned out to be the proving ground, for the basic truth I'd picked up in Washington . . . and tossed onto the floor of the cab right away, being in no mood then for basic truths of any kind.

All I wanted to do was get home before the thunder and lightning broke, get a shower and relax in coolness and quiet. So I tossed the match book onto the floor of the taxi, and that ended that. Who wrote "Death is the Devil's Stronghold" or why, I have no idea. Its only importance is that it was a first signpost, in a way, on a long and uncertain road.

The second was waiting inside my front door, lying on the hall table—Air Mail, Special Delivery. It was a dusty pink envelope post-marked Beverly Hills, addressed in a dashing hand that I recognized at once. I didn't quite toss it on the hall floor, but I wasn't in any mad rush to open it. Lucille Gannon's entire life was Air Mail, Special Delivery . . . a head of lettuce as urgent as the Graeco-Turkish loan, her three marriages contracted and broken and contracted at such breakneck speed, and with such heartless opportunism, or so I'd thought, that it was always a wonder to me her first two husbands were as cut up by her successive departures as they'd been. Her third, George Gannon, an independent producer in Hollywood, seemed made of more lasting stuff, so far.

Put my packages on the table and went along to the sitting room off my brick-walled garden. Outside was that unreal glow that comes just before the sun gives up and lets the thunder and the lightning take over. The leaves were already quivering, and downstairs I could hear Lilac, my colored cook, grumbling to Sheila the Irish setter. It seemed to me a perfectly normal late afternoon in Washington as I opened the lipstick-smeared flap of Lucille Gannon's letter.

Perhaps it should have done so, but the "Darling—you *must* come out here" didn't at all prepare me for what followed.

"Gee Gee has explained you to the Casa del Flores, so you can wire them for a room reservation unless you want to stay with us."

Gee Gee I knew was her latest husband, whom I'd never met. I assumed the Casa del Flores was a hotel. Why I had to be explained in order to get a room in it was confusing. It was not as confusing as the next sentence. I read it twice before I believed I was seeing it properly.

"Your first-born, whom I love and adore, is making a complete and utter and absolute ass of himself, and with the worst little trollop that ever hit Hollywood and Vine."

I thought it must be the heat, for a moment. My first-born was Bill—William A. Latham, aged twenty-two. He was across the room now, on top of my desk, looking at me with a broad grin out of a photo of himself in his white sailor suit before he became a fledgling ensign. It was only a picture, but it was Bill—the grin and the "How do I look, Ma?" scrawled across one corner . . . not handsome but a straightforward honest kid, as little likely to be making an ass of himself over anything as anybody I could imagine. So I wasn't so much surprised as angry. I think it was the grin on his face, up there across the room, that kept me from tearing the letter in bits then and there. But I thought better of it, after I'd cooled off a little, and started at the beginning. And when I'd finished, I wasn't either as angry or as sure as I'd been before. In fact it did look pretty much as if my first-born really was, to all intents and purposes, doing precisely that. Whether it was only in connection with the worst little trollop wasn't entirely clear. The trollop's name, at any rate, seemed to be Doreen McShane, and according to Lucille Gannon's letter if I didn't get out there, fast, it was going to be Doreen Latham, and moreover Bill would be in prison and I'd be in the poorhouse—all before the cock crowed for another morn.

I sat there looking across at Bill and at the pigeon-hole with his letters, letters grown very thin recently. There'd been no mention of Doreen in them, only the course in aeronautical engineering he said he was sweating at, and would it be all right if he sold another Savings Bond as living was expensive. I sat there, almost a drowning man, or at least with a lot of my life flashing in front of me . . . beginning with the plane that reached and stopped at the point of no return, leaving me with two small boys and nobody but Lilac to help bring them up. They were born, as I was, in the house there on P Street, and they'd gone away to school early because I didn't want them to grow up what Lilac calls "spoilrotten," with a couple of women waiting on them. I hadn't married, largely because it seemed to me I had problems enough as it was, and nobody ever appeared that Lilac entirely approved of. And no one worried about it until Colonel

John Primrose (92nd Engineers, U. S. Army, Retired) and his self-styled "functotum," Sergeant Phineas T. Buck (likewise), appeared in our lives one summer at April Harbor on the Chesapeake and changed them completely.

Up to then, for one thing, I'd known nothing about murder, violent death and their investigation, which is their present chief concern, and up to then nobody had cared whether I married or not. Nobody had ever said "Don't you think, Grace dear, you really ought to marry him? Hasn't this gone on long enough, dear . . . ?" Not until Colonel Primrose came along. And still nobody's ever explained what I'd do with Sergeant Buck. You can't lightly sever a man and his shadow. At least I'd thought I couldn't. Now I was wondering. Maybe if I'd had one or both of them in the house, Bill would have learned something Lilac and I and a series of school-masters couldn't teach him. Certainly if he'd learned about women from Sergeant Buck he wouldn't have touched one with a fifty-foot pole. Maybe Lilac and I hadn't done as good a job as we'd thought.

I heard her heavy step on the basement kitchen stairs. She came to the door and stopped, apparently not having heard me come in. "You jus' sittin' here, the trees all sheddin' darkness," she said. "You mus' ain' feelin' well.—Who that come from?"

"From Mrs. Gannon."

Lilac makes on occasion a sound between a sniff and a snort that's as damning as all improper words in the language and like them can't be written down.

"She always got somethin' to say," she added. "What she say now?"

I read the letter to her. With the thunder crashing and the light-ning sizzling around, it was a sort of Wagnerian prelude, with a non-Nordic Lilac taking her cue the instant I'd finished.

"You ain' even thinkin' about goin' out there."

I didn't know what I was thinking. I hadn't got that far.

"Ain' no use to go all that way, child," she said. "If Bill goin' to make a fool out of his-self, he goin' to. If he got wild oats, he got to sow. As ye sow so shall ye reap. That's what the preacher say."

"He doesn't say you have to marry them," I said.

"If his mind's set on marryin', Mis' Grace, ain' nothin' you goin' to say goin' to get it off."

She stood looking at me for a moment before she went over to the telephone. I didn't think about who she might be calling until I heard her voice, sweet as honey and smooth as owl's grease.

"Mr. Buck? How you, sir? Is th' Colonel there? You tell him to get his-self over here quick. The madam, she bent on makin' trouble if somebody don' stop her."

I suppose that's why I went.

It's only when Lilac is being bitterly satirical that she calls me the madam. With Colonel Primrose on her side, both of them badgering me, I didn't have much chance to think . . . not even when Sergeant Buck turned out to be on my side, which in itself should have given me pause.

He appeared the afternoon I was to take my plane, the last word in spit and polish, even to the gold snake stickpin with ruby eye in the discreet white-spotted black tie he reserves for special occasions, usually at Arlington. He spoke the way he does, out of one side of his lantern jaw, the other side immovable as giant granite.

"I just want to say, ma'am, you shouldn't ought to pay no mind to what the Colonel says. He don't understand what it is to be a mother."

I must have looked a little startled. Somehow I hadn't thought of it quite in those terms.

"Or if you don't want to leave the Colonel, ma'am, just say the word. I'll find out who Bill's fraternizing with, and if it looks off-color, ma'am, just give me the office. I'll pick him up and bring him back by the seat of his bri——"

He broke off, his iron deadpan suffused a rich copper. No doubt "britches" is hardly an expression fit for a mother's ears. Equally, no doubt, Sergeant Buck could be as good as his word. He could have picked up the Colossus of Rhodes by less than that.

"I'd better go myself, thank you," I said hastily.

"Okay, ma'am." Sergeant Buck got to the door. "No offense meant, ma'am," he said.

"And none taken, Sergeant," I replied. That, between us, was the *plus grande politesse*. But I was glad I'd never married his Colonel. If anyone was to take my son by the seat of his britches, Ma was the one to do it.

CHAPTER TWO

I REGISTERED at the Casa del Flores in Franklin Canyon at 3:30 Wednesday afternoon, Gee Gee having apparently explained me adequately.

"There's a message for you, Mrs. Latham," the clerk said.

It was from Lucille Gannon, scribbled at top speed on a piece of hotel stationery. "Gone to Palm Springs, dear. Back tomorrow. Do nothing—absolutely nothing—till I see you. Terribly important."

I was hardly surprised there wasn't any word from Bill Latham. I'd wired him at his boarding house in Pasadena, not having a list of the local night spots. Until he should happen to turn up to attend a class or two, it was unlikely he'd find out who he had on his trail. It was equally unlikely, I saw, that I'd run into him at the Casa del Flores. I saw that as I looked at the right-hand side of the menu presented me by a lanky, large, sandy-haired cheerful young man when I called Room Service for a sandwich and coffee before I started to unpack. No matter what was going on, I didn't see how Bill could afford to spend much time in precincts so economically exclusive as these appeared to be.

What I'd expected a Hollywood hotel to look like I don't know, unless it was the plush gold-leaf, black marble job a friend had told me about where they'd spent a stupefying night once. The Casa del Flores was nothing like that. One story high, it rambled in small secluded cottage units just below the rim of the Canyon, through a fairyland of flowers and trees. It was glistening white and enchantingly simple, with an unaffected friendliness that extended even to the bellboys and waiters, often the most snobbish of mankind.

I was aware of it first in the young man waiting to take my order. He was sunburned and freckle-faced, with a cleft chin and big ears and smile-wrinkles fanshaped at the corners of his blue eyes. The sleeves of his starched white coat hit about an inch above hairy bony wrists and his big capable hands looked as though they ought to be doing more productive work than carrying dishes around a Hollywood hotel. I forgot I'd been tired as I gave him my order, and

8

instead of lying down I stepped through the open french windows onto a sun-bleached patio that seemed to belong to me alone. There was a white wrought-iron chaise longue on it, and a table and cushioned chairs. A gorgeous shower of fuchsia in full bloom hung down the whitewashed brick walls on either side. Across the end was an iron railing in front of stone steps going down to the terrace garden below. There was a long vista down the Canyon to where the city lay, shrouded and invisible through its overlying haze. Above the Canyon the sky was a clear almost Mediterranean blue. And it was cool. I stood there almost forgetting why I'd come, until I heard the sudden rap on my room door.

It seemed miraculously quick service. Just the prospect of seeing that grinning freckled face made me smile as I stepped back across the patio into the room. I said "Come in," took off my hat and went across to the closet to put it away. The door opened as I started to reach up to the high shelf . . . but there was no grinning freckled face in the mirror that panelled the door into the next suite, directly opposite the hall door. What I saw in it was a girl, a girl with the most violently sultry pair of grey-blue eyes I've ever seen in all my life. The pointed determined chin, flushed high cheekbones and slender erect body were all of a piece, and it was a piece of five feet two inches of sheer unadulterated tiger-cat. She had a flowing mane of tawny hair. The mandarin spears at the ends of her long sunbrowned fingers looked as if she'd already ripped something open, and as I stared at her in the mirror there was little doubt in my mind that that was precisely what she wanted to do with me.

She'd have done well in the jungle. I saw that by the way she moved in and shut the door swiftly and noiselessly behind her. A leopard skin would have been more suitable for her at the moment than the short white butcher's jacket she had on. Below it was a narrow strip of white bathing suit printed with brown and green flowers, and below that a pair of slim, straight brown legs. Her whole body was quivering. The little lady was more than in a rage. And at me.

"*You!*"

It came out as I put my hat up on the closet shelf and turned back into the room.

"*You!*"

She blazed it out a second time.

"You listen to me. You thought you could sneak in here and nobody know it. Don't fool yourself! We knew you were coming. We knew you'd show up, and don't think we aren't ready for you! I'm not to let you talk to me, but that doesn't keep me from talking to you, and I'm going to, plenty!"

There seemed to be no doubt of it. And to say I was astonished is not enough. I stood there like an oaf.

She made a sound that I suppose could be called a laugh.

"You don't even recognize me. Well, I'm Molly McShane. *Not* Doreen. I've dropped that. It's Molly now, and you're not going to come out here and mess up my life! You're going back where you came from and stay there! You're not going to wreck us——"

There's no use going on saying I was in a daze. Somewhere in the course of it I managed to get my voice, at least.

"Stop it!" I said. "Stop it at once. Who . . . how did you know I was here?"

"How did I know?"

She thrust one brown hand into the pocket of her jacket and pulled out an oblong card. She gave it a defiant flip. It landed on the carpet midway between us—written side up, fortunately. If I'd had to bend down to pick it up what dignity I'd kept would have been badly impaired.

"Molly," it said. "She's come. She's in 102. Better get set.—Sheep."

I said, "Oh." I couldn't think of anything else. It seemed to be me. My room number was 102, and I'd certainly come. Who "Sheep" could be I had no idea at all.

"Listen," the girl said. "I'm not fooling."

It hadn't occurred to me, not remotely, that she was.

"We don't owe you *anything*. You've never done a *thing* for us."

That was a little startling, even if I don't belong to the Sergeant Buck school, which holds that mothers are a special and holy breed. It was not as startling as what she flayed me with next.

"*You! You'd* never have known I was alive if I hadn't begun to get somewhere on my own! *You* didn't help me. *You* didn't give a damn what happened to me! You're not going to step in and use me now. You don't get one cent out of me and not one line of publicity, or anything else . . . we'll see you in hell first! We know your game and we're giving you till noon tomorrow. Get that! *Packed and out* by noon tomorrow! Gee—you make me laugh!"

That was her exit line, and it didn't make me laugh. The scorn and contempt in it, the toss she gave her tawny head, left me staring at the door, wondering if I was in normal possession of my senses.

I looked down to the rug at my feet. The card was still there. I bent down and picked it up. Sheep's message was still on it—or I could still have thought I'd dreamed up the whole thing. I turned it over. On the other side, in the same neat print, it said,

1 chicken sandwich (no mayonnaise)
1 coffee (no cream)

It was a waiter's check. The room number was 102. It was my order. Sheep was my lanky sandy-haired waiter.

Out in the hall I could hear footsteps, then a tap on the door. I slipped the check under the desk blotter and said "Come in." He came, cheerful and debonair as if he had never in all the world written the message that had unleashed the baby hellcat.

"Sorry I was so long," he said. "We've had more late lunches than usual. Where would you like this? Here by the windows?"

He couldn't have been more cordial if I'd been an honored guest in his own home.

"I hope you'll like it here. This is one of the nicest hotels in town. Are you going to stay with us a while?"

It sounded innocent, I thought . . . or was he just checking up for the little lady?

"I'm not sure how long I'll be here," I said.

"I'll take your breakfast order tonight, if you like. We work a staggered shift. I'm on this evening and tomorrow morning, until noon."

I thought there was a short pause before my ominous deadline. I looked around at him involuntarily. He was certainly not my idea of a hatchet man. Still, stranger things have happened in less strange parts of the world.

"Well, I hope you enjoy your lunch, madam."

I dare say my ears had begun by now to detect sinister implications where none existed. At any rate, I think I was on the point of examining my sandwich for a few snowy flakes of arsenic when the phone ringing at the head of the green-and-yellow day bed interrupted me. It was Bill—he'd finally got my telegram. I was so sure of it, and so sure everything would be fine now, that I dashed across the room.

"Hello," I said. "Hello." I waited a moment, and spoke again. It was an open connection, and someone was at the other end. I could hear him breathing . . . a heavy breath, drawn, released, drawn again . . . a strange rasping sound coming at measured intervals in my ear.

"Hello!" I said, sharply this time. "Who is this?"

There was no answer, only the regular wheezing breath, drawn and released into my ear. Then I heard a soft click, and the phone went dead. I stood holding it in my hand, a chilly pricking sensation crawling up and down my spine. It was extremely unpleasant. Then the hotel operator switched in.

"Were you cut off, Mrs. Latham?"

"Yes, I think so," I said. "Where did the call come from?"

"I'm sorry, it was from outside. They'll call again, I expect."

She was right. They called four times within the next hour, in the same way each time . . . a formless invisible figure breathing into my ear, silently ringing off each time I started to speak. The third and fourth time I was increasingly reluctant to answer, but I didn't dare not, in case it was my wretched first-born.

But it was the rock that was the most disquieting. It came between the third and fourth phone call. I was in the bathroom unpacking my toilet case when I thought I heard a sound in the room. I came out, not quickly but with the deliberate caution befitting a woman with a decent sense of the importance of her own preservation. There was no one there. The door into the hall was still closed, and the mirrored door beside my fireplace, which led into the next apartment, was firmly locked. The room it led into had an occupant who was in residence, and also in what sounded like an acute stage of bronchial pneumonia, but the sound of coughing I heard then wasn't what had disturbed me. I went to the coffee table where my tray still was and looked out the long open window, and then I saw it.

It was a jagged rock, lying on a flagstone at the foot of the chaise longue. A paper was tied around it with a piece of ordinary brown string. I glanced at the flower-screened walls, and at the filigreed iron railing connecting them across the end of the patio. The rock could have come from any of the three directions—from either of the adjoining patios or from the terraced porch below. Wherever it came from, however, I didn't much like it.

I went out, reluctantly, to get it, and it was when I bent down to pick it up that the telephone rang for the fourth time. For the fourth time I answered it, to hear nothing but the asthmatic breathing, and the soft click when I started to speak. The only other sound was my neighbor coughing in her room. I picked the rock up again, untied the string and took the paper off. It was a piece of Casa del Flores stationery, slightly soiled. The message on it was printed too, but not neatly as the one signed "Sheep" had been. It was short and to the point:

"Go home. We mean what we say."

CHAPTER THREE

THERE WAS NO DOUBT about that in my mind, not by this time. They'd entirely convinced me. I say "they," because the rock from inside the hotel or its grounds, and the phone calls from outside, plus Miss McShane in person, seemed to indicate at least three people, not counting "Sheep," each with a singularly one-track mind. They wanted somebody to go home. They thought it was me. How long before they would adopt more determined tactics, how long it would take them to find out they were making a fundamental mistake in identification, I had no grounds to work on. I only hoped the latter would occur before the former . . . and before noon the next day. Of course, it was a purely personal point of view.

I tried to explain it the fourth time the phone rang.

"Look . . . you're making a very stupid mis——"

The receiver clicked quietly down at the other end. Before I had time to put the phone down there was a rap at my door. Outside I heard a man's voice.

"Hey, Sheep—pick up the table in Mrs. Ansell's room, will you, boy? She wants to work and I'm loaded up."

"Okay, will do, soon as I get my tray."

My waiter came on in. "May I take your tray now?"

His happy grin was unchanged. Hatchet man or no hatchet man, he certainly seemed to bear me no personal malice. If he noticed the rock, or thought it an odd thing to be lying on the glass table top, he gave no sign of it. He put the napkin over the tray, picked it up and started back to the door. As he opened it, my next door neighbor went into another paroxysm of coughing.

"Gee, poor Mrs. Ansell," he said soberly. "She's sure got it, hasn't she? Had it ever since she came out.—She's a writer," he added by way of explanation.

If she was a writer, she could certainly think up something better than the note thrown into my patio, so I dismissed the idea I'd had that it could have come from her side of the wall. I further dismissed it when I heard her laughing a moment later. In fact, if it hadn't been for the private background acquired in the hour and a quarter I'd been there, I would have thought the Casa del Flores was the most charming and friendly hotel I'd ever been in. It certainly was the quietest—at that time of day and when Mrs. Ansell wasn't coughing.

The quiet had a curious eeriness for me, however, as I waited for the phone to ring again. I looked at my watch. It was a quarter to five—a little late for me to set out to go to my son's boarding house, even if there was any chance of finding him there . . . as, according to Lucille Gannon's letter, there wouldn't be. I took the letter out of my bag and read it again. Reduced to its specific terms, the grounds on which my first-born was making the complete and absolute ass of himself were night spots, gambling hells and bad company, of which Doreen—now Molly—McShane was first and chief. I read over the part that called her the worst little trollop that ever hit Hollywood and Vine, and wondered. Somehow it didn't seem quite the term for her. And what grounds Lucille Gannon had for calling her that, or saying she wanted to marry Bill Latham, weren't stated. What she did state was that Bill was drinking, gambling, throwing money hand over fist down various and assorted night-spot drains, cutting classes and doing no work of any kind. So much I'd told Lilac and Colonel Primrose. I hadn't told either of them that Lucille Gannon also said he had a hot rod and was bound and determined to kill himself. And if all that wasn't disturbing enough, there was something else. What, Lucille didn't say. It was so disgraceful, I'd be so upset, that she didn't feel she could tell me; I had to come and see for myself. So, considering what she did feel free to tell me, and considering each day's crop of new horrors committed by the young and by the returned veterans, I was a lot more worried than I cared to admit even to myself. And nothing had happened since I'd arrived at the Casa del Flores to reassure me. What he was doing now, where he was— what drain, what gambling hell, my wandering child was at . . . it seemed to me the less I thought about it, the better off I'd be. The thing for me to do was wait till he showed up, or until he didn't show up. Or until Lucille Gannon showed up. And while I waited, to bolt my doors until Molly McShane, Sheep and their two friends found out who it was they were really looking for. That was immediate and pressing.

I bolted the door. At least I locked it, and I locked the screen at the french window onto the patio. Then I went back into the bathroom to continue my interrupted packing. I was almost through when the phone rang again. This time I decided I'd let it ring. I could hear that evil breathing in my ear without moving from where I was. It rang a long time, and when I came out to get another bag to unpack it rang again. I had to answer it this time—the rasping breath was better than the persistent jangle going on and on. But it wasn't the asthmatic breather, it was the switchboard operator.

"Oh, Mrs. Latham," she said pleasantly. "Bill called just now. He said to call till I got you, and tell you he's on his way over from Pasadena. He wants you to have dinner with him."

I was so relieved I could have wept . . . relieved that it was finally Bill, relieved not to hear that ghastly silence.

"How long will it take him to get here?"

"Oh, about half an hour. He's got his hot rod."

I had a horrible picture of him, shooting his way through traffic, arriving, like Pretty Boy Floyd, bleeding but triumphant, at his mother's doorstep . . . or of myself identifying him, in case he didn't get there, at the local morgue. That, of course, was before I knew what a hot rod was, and if I'd known it was a hopped-up jalopy that could make a hundred miles an hour I'd have been even more out of mind. And it was only after I'd put the phone down that it occurred to me the switchboard girl had called him "Bill," and seemed to know him quite as well as I did. But sufficient to the day are the evils thereof, and I finished unpacking and hanging up my clothes.

I hadn't, until I heard running footsteps in the hall and a bang-bang on my door, really realized what it was I'd built up from Lucille Gannon's letter. It was a sort of Picture of Dorian Gray, I saw now. I put my hand on the doorknob and paused. On the other side of the door was my first-born. Heaven only knew what it was I expected him to look like, trailing his robes of dissipation and sin. I opened the door, and there he was.

"Ma! Oh, gee, Ma! This is swell!"

"Oh, Bill!" And when he'd let go of me I pushed him back. "Let me look at you! You *rat*—what have you been doing?"

He stood off grinning at me. "Gee, we didn't think you'd *come*, Ma! My letter was just a flier we took. Thanks, Ma! Gee, you're swell!"

I looked blankly at my son. "Letter? What letter?"

Not that it mattered. What mattered was that Bill was still Bill. There were no baggy pouches under his hazel eyes, no loose sagging corners to his wide grinning mouth, no smell of the grog shop or the gin mill—just the same straight-forward, not handsome but for my money pretty attractive young guy who stood six feet, clear-skinned, sunbrowned and lean, clean-cut and clear-eyed, his lightish brown hair bleached and crisp, looking as if he combed it with a rotary eggbeater, and not a delinquent or psychopathic bone in his body so far as I could see.

"What letter, angel?" I asked again. "All the letters I've got from you lately . . ."

I stopped. He was looking at me, as blank as I was.

"Didn't you get my letter, Mother?"

When he calls me Mother it's a matter of some importance.

"Then what . . . I mean, what's the idea? What made you come out here when . . . I mean, look, Mother!"

His seriousness pulled itself in another notch. "Did somebody *tell* you to come out? Was it . . . it wasn't Eustace, was it, by any chance?"

I could tell from the way he asked it that he didn't really believe it was Eustace, whoever Eustace was.

"I don't know Eustace. I've never heard of him," I said.

"Sure you do. Eustace Sype."

I shook my head.

"Are you sure, Mother? Because he says he knows you. That's

how we got to know him so well. He said he was an old friend of yours, in Washington."

"Oh," I said. "Oh yes, of course."

"No likee heem, Eustace Sype?"

He was watching me intently.

"I haven't seen him for a thousand years, sweetie," I said. I could have said that another thousand would be perfectly agreeable to me and that it was the "Eustace" that threw me off. We never called him "Eustace." We called him Stinky . . . Stinky Sype. So far as I know, none of his contemporaries ever called him anything else. After he wrote his autobiographical first novel called *The Coming of Age of E. P. S.* we never called him anything. It was a picture of him and his friends in the roaring Twenties, all of them thinly disguised except Eustace who was completely disguised as hero. We were all a loathsome lot, except Stinky. He was fine, sensitive and cruelly put upon—a lonely spirit struggling for the purer dew of the mountain tops. It was sweet of him to remember me now.

"Is he a friend of yours?" I asked.

"Sure," Bill said. "He's been swell to us. We ran into him in the Pacific. He was the V. I. P. with a road show Special Services brought around. He told us to be sure and look him up. He's got a honey of a place here—we use his swimming pool."

He looked at me questioningly. "And I didn't think it would be him. Was it a dame, Mother? Did some dame get you on our trail?"

"What do you mean by 'our' trail?"

I asked it as casually as I could, but to my surprise his face brightened.

"The big Sheep. You've seen him. Sheep Clarke—he's your waiter. He called me at the lab and said you'd come. I wouldn't have got your wire till I got home at seven. *You've* seen Sheep."

"Yes," I said. "I've seen Sheep. Is *he* a friend of yours, too?"

"Oh, Sheep's my pal. Sheep's tops. He and I were shipmates. Sheep's a right guy, Ma. You'll be nuts about him."

"Good," I said.

I didn't add anything. His enthusiasm for Sheep was too warm and too spontaneous for me to start right away asking him why, if Sheep was such a right guy, and knew who I was, he'd turned Miss McShane loose on me. And I didn't want to bring up the little McShane. I thought others had better bring her up—not me.

His face had sobered again. "But come on, Ma—come clean. Did somebody give you a sob story about us? Because you've got to be on our side, Mother. That's why we wrote you. We need you—boy, do we need you! You see, just as everything gets set, this dame sticks her snoot in, and we're damned if we're going to take it. We tried to explain in the letter, but we didn't want to worry you——"

"Who is this 'we'?" I asked again. "You and Sheep still?"

He grinned at me. "No. All three of us cooked that up. Molly was supposed to mail it. That was about a week ago.—But if you didn't get it, and it wasn't this dame I'm talking about that told you, why, I guess you don't know who our Molly is, do you, Ma?"

He grinned again. "I mean, mine and Sheep's. She belongs to us, and this dame's going to get her dirty mitts chopped off at the elbow if she doesn't keep 'em off our girl."

CHAPTER FOUR

ONE THING at least seemed clear to me at this point, if only one. It didn't take much mental effort to figure out who it was Molly McShane had thought I was. It was relieving, in a sense; it cleared up the little matter of Sheep's note. He'd meant me, and Molly had jumped to another conclusion. But if anything else was clear, it had escaped me. Bill evidently didn't know "this dame's" name, for one thing, or he'd have used it, and for another thing Molly McShane quite evidently didn't know what she looked like.

"—Who was it, Ma?" Bill demanded again. "What made you come out? I mean, it must have been something . . ."

"It was, angel," I said. "A friend of mine wrote me. She seemed to have the idea you were going to hell, jet-propelled. Also not doing any work. It was Lucille Gannon."

"Oh, Cripes. Lucille Gannon. She gives me a pain. The hell I'm not doing any work—we're both on the Dean's List. That's not what she's beefing about, Mother. It's her Gee Gee. That's her beef . . . and our mistake."

He gave me a sardonic and rueful grin.

"I guess we're just boys from the country. We figured she'd want to help out—Molly's under contract to her husband and the best bet he's got. But boy! were we crazy. She hit the ceiling. We gathered the less Gee Gee sees of Molly, even if it costs him money, the better Lucille's going to like it. And how."

"She didn't mention her husband, dear," I said.

"She wouldn't. But that's the dope. You'd think she'd have more sense than to try to get her hooks into Molly."

I wondered whether he might not have something. Lucille's letter about his moral dissolution could easily enough be a smoke screen to cover what she thought was really her own husband's wayward trail. She might have thought that if I came out and raised holy hell it would scare Gee Gee back into harness. But it's hard to confine an irrational woman in a rational pattern, so I had no idea really what was in her mind.

The broad grin came back to Bill's face. "Let me tell you about the little Moll. Did you see 'Farewell My Life'?"

I shook my head.

"Well, she was in that. George Gannon produced it. She was mostly on the cutting-room floor, but that was because the star put up such a beef . . . George was afraid she'd walk out of the new picture he was making."

He was genuinely indignant. I waited, trusting that if I sat tight and listened carefully, sooner or later something that was simple and comprehensible would come out of this mare's nest.

He relaxed then and grinned at me again. "You see, Ma, Molly McShane's our girl."

"So you said," I observed. "I'm still a little fuzzy."

"I mean we've got a deal." He began to laugh. "Me and Sheep. We've got a deal. We're star-makers."

"You're what?" I demanded.

"Star-makers. We're making a star out of Molly McShane. And she's a honey, Ma—you'll love her. Now wait a minute—don't go Eastern or maternal on us. I promised 'em you wouldn't. So you've got to wait till you see her. She's got *everything*."

"I'm going to see her some time?"

"Sure, tonight. It's my night to take her out. It's Sheep's night on."

I looked at him blankly. That seemed to amuse him too.

"Didn't la Gannon tell you? I'm a waiter here. Sheep and I work a staggered shift. We figured it was a neat way to meet a lot of the big shots. You know they like to be democratic. All kinds of people come here, glad to give you a hand because you're a waiter and going to school, that wouldn't let you past the front desk if you tried to see 'em at the studios. You'd be surprised——"

"I wouldn't be surprised at anything, any more," I said. "All I'd like to do is find out what you're talking about. Why don't you begin at the beginning? I'll try not to go maternal and Eastern on you."

"Okay. I wish old Sheep was here."

He disappeared into the hall and came back in a moment with Sheep, apparently materialized out of thin air except that he was carrying a table, on it the most extraordinary assortment of raw vegetable matter . . . some whole and recognizable, some grated and partly so, some juiced and not recognizable at all. An herbivorous animal was clearly in residence at the Casa del Flores, maybe the Yearling in person.

Sheep put the table down and came in. "Hello, Mrs. Latham. It's swell of you to come out here to help us——"

He stopped as Bill kicked him in the shin, his freckled face getting redder and his grin more sheepish by the second.

"—She didn't get our letter. Lucille wrote to her about us—she's come to rescue us from sin and vice. Wait till she finds out what we're really in."

Sheep turned a still deeper brick red. His sleeves seemed to have shrunk another inch.

"But first we've got to tell her about Molly."

Sheep nodded earnestly. "It's like this, ma'am. We were in Galveston . . ."

He sounded a little like Sergeant Buck, the only other person who calls me "ma'am," but this time it was only Texas.

"And we got plastered one night, Ma."

While the solid vegetables wilted and the liquid ones precipitated in the bottom of their glass, I heard the story. And reduced to some kind of order, the facts were simple if fantastic. They got plastered. They met a girl who took them to a juke box joint that ran amateur talent shows. That night the hot number was Doreen McShane. They wanted another girl, but Doreen's mother was there. They couldn't have been too plastered, or at least they managed someway

to convince Mrs. McShane they had important Hollywood connections. It was a dilapidated, white-bearded gag of such crippled
antiquity that they never expected to be taken seriously . . . and
when they woke up next morning, Doreen and her father were
downstairs in the hotel lobby.

They thought of the fire escape, but there wasn't one. Then they
remembered they did have Hollywood connections—they knew Eustace Sype. Furthermore, Bill knew Mrs. George Gannon. They
knew one or two others, including stars of greater or less magnitude,
who'd sweated it out on rain-drenched coral islands entertaining the
Navy and the G. I.'s and who might or might not remember them.
They had a pretty impressive bankroll between them, thanks to their
aviators' pay, no dependents and usually abstemious habits. They
took a cold shower and went downstairs with a deal cooked up, depending on what Doreen McShane's father was like and what Doreen
looked like in the light of day. And her father was sweet and sort of
pathetic, and Doreen looked fine. In fact, Doreen looked wonderful
. . . young, and scared, and wonderful.

"And you forgot to mention all this when you were home on
terminal leave," I said.

They both grinned.

"We were plenty scared ourselves," Bill said. "We didn't know
how we were going to swing it. You see, they believed us. We'd
have felt like dirty dogs to . . . well, you know. It was more than
a good gag, by that time. But it sure takes a lot of dough to keep
a gal in the right places where the right people can see her with the
right clothes on. We wouldn't have got to first base if we hadn't
taken Eustace Sype in on it."

"And you wait, Mrs. Latham," Sheep added. "She's not just
cheesecake and cream. She's got something. She can *act*. Can't she,
Bill?"

Bill agreed she could. And they were going to show me. That
set them off again. If anything was so hilariously amusing as they
seemed to think all this was, I dare say it was worth it.

"She's going to put on an act for you, Mrs. Latham," Sheep said.
"She knows you're here. We weren't going to tell you. We wanted
you to see she really can act. It's something Bill dreamed up——"

He was interrupted by an angry bellow, a violent one-man up-
heaval, out in the tiled hallway.

"Waiter! Where's my order! *Sheep!*"

The herbivorous client was plainly impatient. Bill jumped to the door. "On your way, boy! It's You Know Who. Got to keep him happy."

He held the door open. Reflected in the mirror across my room, dancing up and down in his own open door, was a roly-poly little man with peeled popped-out brown eyes. He looked like an irate pygmy on the warpath compared to the two six-footers now rushing his sustenance to him . . . though few pygmies would have had the courage of his sartorial convictions. Electric blue slacks and a plum-colored shirt with short sleeves, open at the neck and with its tail hanging out, made him a startling figure. He was gesticulating with a cigar chewed to soggy shreds at one end and stone cold at the other. He hadn't shaved for some time, and there was much more black bristly hair on his face than had ever been recently on his shiny barren pate.

"I call!" he shouted. "I wait! What happens? Nothing! This, I don't like!"

He jammed his cigar into his mouth and jerked it out again.

Bill hastily pulled my door shut. Through it I could hear him and Sheep pouring on oil and soothing syrup.

You Know Who, I gathered, was a person of considerable importance, whose name was not to be bandied loosely about. When Bill came back he didn't mention it. He was looking at his watch.

"Gee, I told her I'd get her at seven," he said. "I'd better shove. She's at the other end of the hotel. Shall I bring her here, or do you want to meet us in the cocktail lounge? I've reserved a table."

"Are waiters allowed to eat with the guests?" I asked.

I saw now why Lucille Gannon had felt it was necessary for Gee Gee to explain me so I could get a room in this exclusive caravanserie. And I supposed also that the terrible thing had been explained . . . the one really unpardonable sin, the thing Bill was doing that was so awful she didn't feel free to tell me and that I'd have to see for myself. Bill was a waiter. That would be like Lucille. Unless, of course, there was something I still didn't know.

"I'm not a waiter till noon tomorrow, Ma. I'm a young man about town tonight. You're in the democratic West now, lady. Anybody's as good as anybody else as long as he's got the dough to prove it."

"All right, sweetie," I said. "I'll meet you in the lounge."

I washed my face and changed my dress. Being relieved at not finding my son wallowing around in dens of vice among the grosser fleshpots, I suppose, I could afford to be amused rather than alarmed at the fantastic nonsense he and his friend Sheep were involved in. Or so I thought at the moment. As for the girl, I was anxious to see her. What kind of an actress she was was going to be shown far better by the ordinary course of events than by any amateur script Bill and Sheep could ever cook up. When she found I wasn't "this dame" who was going to get her dirty mitts chopped off at the elbow, she was going to need to be some actress!

CHAPTER FIVE

THE COCKTAIL LOUNGE was back along the flower-bordered flagstone path in the main group of low white stuccoed buildings surrounding a small central patio. The glass doors opened into a narrow foyer with walls of eggplant-tinted glass, the dining room on the left, the lounge on the right. A wood fire was burning in a huge ranch-type fireplace on one side, with maidenhair fern and orchids and showering begonias growing from niches in the rock chimney-breast. The rest of the room was chartreuse and lemon-yellow, the rugs, the intimate leather seating compartments softly lighted from behind the cornice at the top of the eggplant-tinted walls. A curving panel of glass formed the side of the room opposite the fireplace, and gave a long lovely view sweeping the whole length of the narrow Canyon. The room was not crowded. Fifteen people or so were standing or seated on high yellow leather stools at the bar curving in around the corner opposite the door. The tables were empty except for one large but pleasantly secluded arrangement, at the left end of the glass wall, that looked like a luxuriously padded semi-circular bathtub. A man's head and a woman's head with shoulders were sticking up out of it, looking around to see who else was there.

The steward belonged to an older school of hotel personnel than the others I'd seen around. If he didn't approve of a waiter's mother being his guest he didn't show it. He led me with the dignity of the presiding bishop to the table Bill had reserved. We had to pass the table in the corner, and as we did I was startled to hear my name.

"Grace! Bless me, my dear! It isn't *actually* you, is it, darling?"

I turned. It was the man in the overstuffed bathtub—though that seems a vulgar thing to call its chartreuse leather elegance—and he was someone I had never laid eyes on before. He was unbelievably fat, with a thin black mustache dripping, Chinese fashion, at either end of his mouth. His brows had an Oriental upward curve, and his eyes were somewhere in the glistening rolls of fat, shining and twinkling. He was very short, so short his elbows could hardly reach the table. He was holding his right hand out to me—the last third of his stubby index finger entirely covered by a carved jade buddha—and still I had never seen him before.

"Grace! It's been years, darling. Years and years and years! Eustace . . . Eustace Sype. Don't tell me you've——"

"Oh," I said. "Hello, Eustace. I didn't recognize you."

"No one ever does, darling. None of my old friends." He shook, as if a subterranean disturbance was causing considerable surface reaction. "I couldn't be the tallest man in the world, so I decided to be the widest. I've done very well, wouldn't you say, dear?"

"Superbly," I said, and with just cause. Still, anything that changed the Stinky Sype I'd known was all to the good. And he had been nice to my son. I thanked him for it.

"Oh, he's divine, Grace! He's a divine young man. The Navy did a first-rate job on him. He's enchanting, dear!" He put his left hand out and closed it over his companion's bejewelled hand. "And you must meet my friend."

His friend, silent and a little watchful up to then, responded with a quick surface smile. She was blond, not young, pretty dazzling, opulently dressed, a sable coat casually drooping from her plumpish black satin shoulders.

"Mrs. Kersey, Grace. Viola Kersey."

Mrs. Kersey's smile switched on and off again. As she started to raise her hand Eustace plopped a hand down on it, fluttering his other toward the door.

"But wait, darling. Here they come. Here are Bill and Molly. Come, darlings—come and join us. We'll all dine here."

I turned quickly. They were just coming in. Some sixth sense told me that Eustace Sype should not be a witness to Molly's meeting and mine. His bright little eyes were too eager. And perhaps it wasn't a sixth sense at all but just a common one, based on the known fact that fat though a leopard may get with good hunting, his spots remain unaltered. Or perhaps it was just the instinctive desire of the female to protect her young, which in my case seemed to have taken on a tripartite division, consisting for the moment of my first-born, his friend the Sheep, and their personally adopted ward the tiger kitten.

Whatever it was, it occurred to me irresistibly to avoid a meeting in front of Eustace Sype and his lady friend Mrs. Viola Kersey. Bill and Molly were still far enough away for me to do it.

"Later, Eustace," I said. "I haven't seen Bill for ages."

I went toward the two of them, so that I was between Molly McShane and Eustace Sype when she first became aware of who I was.

"—Mother, here she is. This is Molly."

Bill was six feet of pride and pleasure. It was very nice. And the girl at his side . . . She didn't stop moving exactly, but her legs seemed to have turned to sticks of wood, and she swallowed, and swallowed again. Her hyacinth-blue eyes had the stunned look a small child's eyes have when it's made a hideous mistake it never meant to make, and knows no possible excuse and no conceivable way out. It wasn't a tiger kitten that was looking at me. It was a little shorn lamb that didn't know which way to turn.

"Hello, Molly," I said. "It's nice to see you."

I put out my hand. Somehow she managed to get her hand up. It was frozen, every nerve in it quaking and quivering.

"Eustace wanted us to join them, but I thought it would be better if we didn't."

"Good," Bill said. He couldn't, being so much taller than the girl, see the agony in her face, or the quick relief at not having to face two more people, but he could feel the wooden hesitation in her body as he took her arm. "What's the matter, Molly? Come on. She won't bite."

Molly McShane moistened her full red lips. They stood out against the chalky whitewashed look of her sunbrowned skin as if they had no proper relation to it. She was scared, scared of what I was going to say and what I must be thinking. Nevertheless she was game about it. She even managed to toss Eustace a gay little gesture as we passed his table. Her voice was still lost even when we sat down; she was still holding her breath, waiting for the thin ice to break. When it didn't, when I said nothing to indicate I'd seen her before or that she'd practically torn me verbally limb from limb, a puzzled disbelief crept into her eyes.

Only once did they meet mine directly, as Bill and I sipped a martini. There was a sudden mute appeal in them that I couldn't interpret. I didn't know whether she was begging me to be silent or to say what I had to say then and there. I thought a cocktail would help her out, but it was tomato juice Bill ordered for her.

"We don't let her drink. She's too young, and anyway it's bad for her skin."

Now that she wasn't in a passion of fury, she did look a lot younger than I'd thought of her as being, and so fragile that I decided they didn't let her eat either. That was before I knew the camera adds its own ten pounds, and one has to be a cadaver in private life not to be a fat lady on the screen. He ordered her a minute steak, however, and it was just as she was recovering enough to treat it as food and not a coiled rattlesnake that I put an abrupt end to everything. It was entirely in the interests of keeping some kind of conversation going, too, because I didn't, at that time, care at all who Eustace Sype was with.

"The woman with Eustace looks familiar to me," I said. It was true, though until I found myself saying it I wasn't conscious of having thought it. "Who is she? Mrs. Kersey, I think he said."

Bill glanced around. Molly was without interest in anything but the steak. "I don't know. She's new to me. Kersey?"

He beckoned to the waiter. "Who's the dame with Mr. Sype?"

The grey-haired waiter leaned over the table. "One of the old-timers. Viola Van Zant, she used to be. Joe'd know her."

Molly McShane had her bite of steak half-way to her mouth. Her hand stopped, her mouth stayed half open, as if she had turned to sudden clay. She shut her mouth and put her fork down. She seemed for a moment to have stopped breathing. She was the little jungle cat again, silent and intent, as wary and watchful as if the wind suddenly shifting had made her aware that the hunter was dangerously close.

The hunter, or the hunted? I couldn't tell, not knowing how much was fear, how much anger. The hyacinth-blue eyes were black, sultry and smouldering again. Her hands moved to her lap. I saw her open her black faille bag. She took out a gold compact the size of a saucer, snapped it open and held it up to her face. She wasn't looking at herself. Her eyes were fixed beyond her own image, the mirror turned so she could see the woman sitting with Eustace Sype.

"He always has some dame in tow," Bill was saying. "You wonder where he picks some of them up. Business is business, I guess."

The name Viola Van Zant had meant nothing to him. It meant something to me. And it seemed to mean a great deal to Molly McShane. She'd closed her compact and put it back in her bag. She was sitting there taut, withdrawn into herself.

Then she moved abruptly. "Excuse me, please, will you, Bill? I've got to go to the Powder Room. I'll be back in just a minute."

Her words were so clipped and breathless that he looked around at her blankly.

"Please, Bill—let me out."

"What's wrong?"

"Nothing at all. Let me out, please."

He moved then, and she was out of the seat and across the room.

"I don't know what's got into her tonight," Bill said. "I don't know what the hell's the matter with her."

"What is the name of this dame you were talking about, Bill?" I asked. "The one you're going to chop off at the elbows? What's her name, and what's she got to do with Molly McShane?"

He looked at me for a long moment, and then, very deliberately, turned in his seat and looked at the woman with Eustace. The two of them had their heads bent together, intently concerned with their own private business. Mrs. Kersey was talking, Eustace listening. Bill turned back. There was something about the set of his jaw that I didn't like.

"Come on," he said shortly. "Let's get out of here. Don't look back. I don't want them to know we're interested. Make it snappy, will you?"

I wished profoundly then that I'd kept my mouth shut. I wished I'd left it all—whatever it was—to Molly McShane.

CHAPTER SIX

WE WENT across the lounge to the foyer. Eustace Sype and Mrs. Viola Kersey were too intent on their own affairs to notice us until we'd passed them. Their eyes followed us then. I could see them watching Bill when he left me in the foyer and went over to the bar to sign the check. Her eyes still on him, Mrs. Kersey was asking a question. When Eustace answered with an elaborate shrug they both laughed, and somehow it didn't look to me like pleasant laughter. Bill was talking to the grey-haired man behind the bar. When he turned, Eustace beckoned to him. He went over to their table and stood there a moment talking to them.

"He wanted us to get Molly and come over to his house for a nightcap," he said when he'd joined me again. "I told him we were busy."

We went outside and down the steps in silence. He seemed to be thinking things over seriously, and I let him think.

"I was talking to Joe, over at the bar," he said then. "He's been around a long time. He was one of the old originals—Keystone cop, Western bad man stuff. Knows every jerk in town."

"Does he remember Viola Van Zant?"

He nodded. "That's the point. He says she was hot stuff—one of the old guard that bit the dust when sound came in. She tried to stick, but no soap. Then a big hunk of dough from Chicago came along and she grabbed him and got out. Joe says she blew in on the Chief this morning. He wanted to bet me a sawbuck she's trying to stage a comeback. She's taken 31-B. That's the best suite in the whole joint—sixty-five smackers per diem, and boy, it's a honey. It's just below you on the bottom terrace. Oh, well."

He shrugged. "She may have been hot stuff in her day but nobody knows it now. Sic transit gloria mundi. They ought to put that in neon lights in every star's dressing room."

"Would she be 'this dame' that you people are so scared of?" I inquired, patiently.

He was silent for a moment.

28

"I know it sounds screwy, Ma." He was making an unsuccessful attempt to be casual about it. "But . . . we don't know *who* she is. We don't know her name. We just know she exists. We didn't know that till a month ago, when we got our first real publicity break for the Moll. She was right on our trail from then on.—And Molly's never seen her. She doesn't know her name either—or she didn't when we were cooking up the deal to try to get you to come out."

He looked at me with a half grin.

"I said it sounded screwy. You'll just have to take our word for it. It's a . . . a sort of blackmail job, in a way, Mother. This dame's got some kind of hold on Molly and her parents. She keeps calling Molly and me and Sheep up long distance, from New York. I mean, it's screwy as hell."

"Well," I said, "I suppose you at least know what she wants."

"Oh, we know that. She wants us and Molly's parents to get out of the picture. She's going to take our little gal over. And I'm damned if I can see how it could be this Viola Van Zant woman. My guess is Molly's just got the jitters. She's been a wreck ever since this started, the poor little devil."

I couldn't tell whether he was dismissing the idea on my account, or whether it was the truth he was telling, or thought he was telling.

"You might have a look-see in the Powder Room," he said. "I'll stroll up to her room, just in case. If you aren't here I'll be along to your room in a jiffy."

We were in the central patio then. It was like a small private walled garden, with a lighted fountain in the middle, and a few other lights discreetly placed among the flowering trees. A pergola ran along the end of the main lobby building, with unobtrusive signs over the doors opening out into it. The first one said "Telephone," the last said "Powder Room."

I didn't expect to find Molly McShane there any more than Bill had expected me to. And I didn't. There was no one there until just as I started to leave. Then a girl burst in. She was blond and slightly dishevelled, and she could have stood rather less to drink than she'd had.

"Is this yours?"

She balanced herself against the door frame and shoved a black faille bag out at me. It was Molly's, the one she'd taken the saucer-sized compact out of to get a look at Mrs. Kersey. Or it was one just like it.

"No," the girl said. "You've got yours. But here, you take it anyway. I found it in the telephone booth, and I'm getting out of here. I don't want some screwy dame to start yelling I lifted her crown jewels. If it's a booby trap they can have it."

She came on in, dropped the bag on the glass-topped table along the mirrored wall, and looked at herself.

"Gee. I look awful, and I feel awful."

She put one hand out to steady herself, and closed her eyes. Then she opened them and looked around.

"What was I doing? Oh, I know. I was calling a taxi. I was going somewhere. I know—I was going home. That's what I was going to do. I was going to get the hell out of here and go home."

She wove out, leaving Molly's bag on the powder-strewn table. I picked it up and brushed it off. I could feel the big round compact through the cloth. If it was a booby trap, it was one in which Molly McShane herself had been caught, in a way. She'd whipped out at top speed, not to go to the Powder Room but to the telephone booth, and it was urgent enough for her to go to the nearest one, and disturbing enough to make her dash off forgetting her bag.

Bill had said she had the jitters, which was obviously the case . . . but it seemed to me, in spite of my son, that even if he and Sheep Clarke did not know the name of their persecutor, Molly McShane appeared to know it very well. She not only knew her name—she knew she was to be in the hotel that day, which was another fact she'd neglected to tell Bill and Sheep. There didn't seem to be much doubt, I thought, that they were much deeper in the dark about the whole thing than their little Moll was.

I thought back to her blistering attack on me. "You'll not get one cent of money out of me, and not one line of publicity. We'll see you in hell first." I wondered. Unlike Bill and Sheep again, Miss Molly McShane appeared to know, exactly and specifically, what "this dame" wanted. That, however, was stranger still. If Mrs. Kersey could wear the clothes and jewels she did, and pay sixty-five dollars a day for a suite of rooms, money of the sort Molly and the two boys had couldn't be expected to interest her. As for the publicity, they seemed to have to work for all they got. If Mrs. Kersey *qua* Viola Van Zant was trying to stage a comeback, she'd chosen very weak reeds to lean upon so far as I could see. Bill was surely right about one angle of it. It was screwy. It was about the screwiest business I'd heard of. Still, this was Hollywood, and I was just a woman from a far countree, where if one found an evening bag left in a hotel telephone booth the idea that it was a booby trap would never remotely present itself.

I put Molly's bag under my arm with my own and went back outside. Bill was nowhere in sight. Mrs. Viola Kersey and Eustace Sype were, however. They were coming down the flagged steps from the lounge. Eustace fluttered his hand at me.

"Oh, Grace! Viola's decided she'll turn in early too. You both go the same way, so I'll leave you together. Come for tea tomorrow, will you, darling? I'll send my chauffeur at five. I don't get up till four. Good night, dear. I'll see you tomorrow.—Not you, Viola. Just Grace. I've seen enough of you tonight, darling. It's nice having you back."

He looked at his wrist watch.

"I must run, darlings. I've got some people waiting for me at home and I'm terribly late. Good night."

"—Isn't he a lamb?"

Mrs. Kersey said it with a warm throaty chuckle.

"He's one of my oldest and dearest friends. Utterly sweet and utterly malicious. I wouldn't trust him around the next corner, unless his own selfish aggrandizement were involved. He simply adores your son Bill."

"I think Bill's fond of him too," I said.

"One is so blind when one is young," said Mrs. Kersey. "One is the victim of so many disabling semantic reactions."

I was the victim of a disabling reaction of some kind myself, if stubbing my toe on a flagstone could be so called. I couldn't have been more surprised. Along with her cultivated voice, the star of the silent screen had picked up the words to go with it. It was startling. I hadn't heard her speak till then, but I'd never have thought of her as zooming along on that conversational level. If she kept it up, I could see why Eustace Sype had had enough of her in one evening.

She stopped and lifted her face to the evening air, and drew a deep savoring breath, her jewelled hand raised, resting lightly on her full bosom.

"Ah, Hollywood! It's so wonderful to be back! Even the air—the soft, lovely air of it—has its memories, Mrs. Latham. Some happy, poignantly happy . . . some sad, poignantly sad. If we could only know. If we could only start our lives at the end, and *know* when we're young, and be innocent and unsullied and ignorant when we're old! Don't you think so, Mrs. Latham?"

"No," I said. "I think it would be horrible. I like the present arrangement."

"Ah, but I'm a romantic, Mrs. Latham. I love romance. Hollywood is so full of romance."

"I believe that's one of the chief complaints about it, isn't it?" I remarked. "And it's probably changed a lot since you were here."

She glanced at me quickly.

"Then you remember me. Oh, how wonderful that is. It's wonderful to be remembered. I've been happy away from here, but never as happy as I once was. My husband tore me away. He said Love is a jealous god. He couldn't share me with a hundred and twenty million people. And I was *so* young! I believed . . . and believing, I left—I left, and went with him."

"Are you back now?" I asked. "I mean are you going back into pictures?"

"I can't decide. Dear Eustace insists, and there's a producer . . . there's always a producer, you know. But I've been so happy just being a simple wife. I can't really decide. But I so love it here. The air is like wine. The wine of life."

She drew another deep and lingering breath of it.

"It's good to be alive, Mrs. Latham. I believe Life is the one great good."

I believed she had something. Most of the other goods were fairly useless without it, anyway. And I hoped she kept it. If she really was who Molly McShane seemed to me, at any rate, to think she was, and had thought *I* was, earlier, she only had until tomorrow noon to do something about it.

I'm not sure Mrs. Viola Kersey didn't sense a certain cynicism in her present audience, however, because she moved on beside me, rather abruptly leaving the Hollywood air to seep into her lungs by ordinary processes.

"Your son said he and Miss McShane were coming to join you," she said.

I'd had the idea that was why she was dawdling. She wanted them to catch up with us.

"I'm so interested in those dear young people," she went on. "Eustace tells me how sweet and how unselfish those boys of yours have been to Miss McShane. It must be *wonderful* to have sons, Mrs. Latham. *I* never *had* a son. It was the great price I had to pay, my dear. Because Hollywood has changed. It's all *so* different. We could have husbands—I had two before my last one, or was it three? —but we couldn't have babies. They were afraid the fans wouldn't approve. But ah, how little they knew! And now, now, Mrs. Latham, on December 31st, they make a New Year's announcement they're going to have a baby the last of September, and never let you forget it. It's *so* sweet, and *so* different. And it's divine of the public—they love vital statistics. It's *sweet*, isn't it, Mrs. Latham?"

I said I supposed it was. It happens not to be one of my major interests. I wasn't really competent to discuss it.

"And Miss McShane. Of course I'm interested in her, too." Mrs. Kersey spoke with less soul and ardour. "I knew her mother. She was a bad and wicked woman, Mrs. Latham."

I looked at her quickly then, and not unstartled, I may say.

"You doubt me," she said. "I see you doubt me, Mrs. Latham. But I *know*. *Believe* me, I know. Wisdom is a rare quality, Mrs. Latham. Perhaps her mother thought she was doing her best . . . but such a place, for a young girl! Eustace told me. Those sweet boys found her in a juke joint. Imagine, Mrs. Latham—that dear child in a *juke* joint!"

She had whipped up such a warmth of devotion for Molly McShane at this point, and was apparently so absorbed in her passion, that it gave me a chance to glance back quickly to see if Molly and Bill were about to head into this, too. They weren't in sight, but someone else was. Even at that distance, and dimly lighted as the patio was, there was no mistaking the figure of Eustace Sype. He was moving not in our direction but in the opposite one, the way Bill had taken to go find Molly. It seems absurd to say he was moving stealthily, but that was definitely the impression he gave. And as if Mrs. Kersey were equipped with eyes in the back of her head, she went on without so much as stopping for a breath after she finished with the juke box joint:

"Is it Eustace you see, Mrs. Latham? Dear Eustace. He's such a rotten liar. He had no possible intention of going home after your son declined his invitation. He was just getting rid of us. Oh, well, I dare say each of us has his own self-reflexiveness, and his own *raison d'être*, Mrs. Latham. It's not for us to judge."

We'd come to the entrance hall that divided my room from the one Sheep had been so long delivering the vegetables to. I'd gathered that the stone staircase there at the left led down to Mrs. Kersey's suite.

"Well, good night, Mrs. Latham." She held out her hand. It was soft and plump and somehow unpleasant to touch, a selfish egotistical sort of hand. "Do tell the boys how much I'm interested in helping them with Miss McShane. I can be of great help, Mrs. Latham. After all, what is money for if one can't use it to help others? I could take so much of their burden——"

"I don't think they feel it's a burden, Mrs. Kersey," I said deliberately. "They seem to think it's fun, and they seem to be doing very well."

"Of course they are, Mrs. Latham. They're doing divinely. But you know how men are. There are so many things they never think of that a girl needs, to make really the most of herself in this extraordinary world. But just tell Miss McShane how much I'm interested in her career. Will you, Mrs. Latham? Thank you, dear. And there's——"

She stopped, listening. "Is that my telephone?"

Her ears were sharper than mine, but I heard it too as it rang again. "It sounds like it," I said.

"I can't think who'd be calling me. No one knows I'm here. Unless it's my husband calling long distance, the dear man. Well, I must run. Good night, Mrs. Latham."

She didn't run. She moved off with the deliberate balanced rhythm of a woman who'd studied to make herself what she was, and who'd rather miss a call from her husband than relax and be natural for a moment.

CHAPTER SEVEN

I STOOD FOR AN INSTANT looking after her. "So," I thought. "She doesn't want to take money from Molly—she wants to give it to her." Molly McShane had guessed wrong again. She seemed to have a talent for it. And I couldn't help but wonder. An apple had been currency in the Garden of Eden . . . what form would it have now that Viola Kersey had cast herself in the serpent's rôle? I glanced back to see if maybe Bill and Molly were finally coming. They'd be interested to know that a proposition was in the making. But no one was in sight . . . no one, that is, except the blond girl I'd met in the Powder Room. She appeared to be wandering around still, hunting her taxi, I supposed, though at the moment she gave more the impression of being headed back toward the bar.

Mrs. Kersey had got to the bottom of her private stone stairway and was going in the door of her cottage when I turned back to go to mine. A light suddenly switched on, and as suddenly off, over the door at the end of her house. I stopped. She was closing the front door behind her. I could see her shadow crossing the broad window behind the venetian blinds. Someone who had been in her apartment was leaving by the patio door. I was sure of that before I heard the creak of an iron hinge. It was a slow, cautious creak, coming from the solid wood gate in the white wall across the walk at the foot of the stairs. I could see the gate move in the light from an old-fashioned street lamp on a vine-covered post at the right of the bottom step.

And suddenly the gate stopped moving. A slim black figure slipped through it, silhouetted against the white stucco, silhouetted just long enough to close the gate as quietly as she'd opened it. It was little Miss Molly McShane. And then it wasn't . . . she disappeared somewhere into the shadow of the terrace wall, as silently as if she were herself a shadow. She had to be down there still, however, I thought, as the stone steps seemed to be the only exit. I moved on into my own hall to give her a chance to come up. I thought briefly of calling to her to tell her I had the evening bag, but that I dismissed. I didn't want her flying at my throat a second time.

Mrs. Kersey's phone was ringing again, muted but audible. As I let myself into 102 I had the same creeping chill down my spine that my own ringing phone had given me that afternoon. I could see Mrs. Kersey picking it up and hearing the same warning asthmatic wheeze . . . unless the tactics had been changed.

I looked over at the table where I'd left the rock that also was meant for her. It was gone. The glass under it had been polished off, the dried soil that had stuck to it neatly wiped away. The maid could have taken it, I thought, though the day bed was still made up and the wastebasket not emptied. Or it could have been whoever had brought the two extravagant bowls of flowers that had come since I went out to dinner. I looked at the cards on them. The bronze chrysanthemums were from Gee Gee and Lucille with love, which seemed to put me on new terms with George Gannon, whom I'd never met. The roses were from Bill. They were on the bamboo coffee table. As I untied the card I saw something black caught at the morticed corner where the bamboo had splintered. It was a small triangular piece of black lace.

I pulled it out and looked at it, and then I looked at the drawer where I'd put Sheep's message to Miss Molly McShane and the one that had come tied to the rock. I went over, laid my bag and Molly's on the chest and the scrap of black lace beside them, and opened the drawer. It was quite empty. Both messages were gone. The coffee table was in a direct line from there to the window looking out onto my patio. Anyone in a black lace and in a hurry to get out could easily not have noticed a fragile pull at her skirt as she went . . . But on the whole it seemed a little silly. She could, of course, figure that removing the evidence left it just my word against hers, if I decided to tell my son and she cared to deny it. It would be ever so easy for Bill to wonder if Ma wasn't cracking up a little bit, maybe . . . or for some reason sticking a monkey wrench in their beautiful deal. Perhaps the child was smarter than I'd thought. She was certainly a busy little eager beaver.

I was thinking that, half amused and half disturbed, when there was a sharp knock on my door . . . a demand, not a request, to open up. It came a second time as I crossed the room. And there she was—Molly McShane, breathless as if she'd been running, blue eyes blazing black and distended, small fists clenched.

"My bag . . . I've lost it. A girl up there says she gave it to a lady. It was in the phone booth. She——"

Her eyes were darting like twin blue-black dragonflies beyond me around the room. She spotted the bag by mine on top of the chest, and like a flash she was past me and across the room. She grabbed it and held it clutched to her midriff, the scrap of black lace fluttering to the floor. She was too excited to see it. She whirled around at me, her quick staccato breathing audible all the way across the room. I closed the door to keep it from being audible across the hall.

"You took it. You know——"

"Of course I took it, Molly," I said. "The girl found it in the telephone booth and brought it to the Powder Room. She gave it to me. I took it to give to you, and you've got it. If you've lost anything out of it, I didn't take it, and I don't think the girl did. It might be a good idea to look and see."

It wasn't a screwy dame yelling that she'd lost the crown jewels, but it was a slightly screwy youngster terrified before she knew whether she'd lost anything or not. Or that was what I thought at the moment.

She ripped open the plastic crystal clasp and looked inside. The relief on her intensely mobile pointed little face was instantaneous. It was followed up as instantly by something else.

"You . . . you read——"

"Look," I said patiently. "I didn't open your bag. I didn't read anything. I didn't *look* in it. I recognized it and I felt your big compact in it. It never occurred to me to open it. I'm not interested in what you carry around. But now you're here there *is* something I'm interested in. Why don't we quit all this play-acting? I've had about all of it I care to take—beginning with this afternoon at half-past three. What *is* all this nonsense, Molly?"

Her body stiffened straight as an arrow, defiance pointing up mistrust and disbelief. I added, before she had a chance to lash out again, "And what *has* Viola Kersey got to do with you?"

She stood staring rigidly at me for a moment. Then—*mirabile dictu* —it was as if I'd sprayed a dusty windshield and wiped a clean rag across it. The whole world was clear and beautiful, as transparent and pure as an early morning in May. All doubt and mistrust vanished. She let go the stranglehold on the bag. Her taut little body melted into a warm lovely curved line, her eyes widened, and she even smiled at me, like a happy child.

"I'm so sorry, Mrs. Latham," she said. "I shouldn't have thought you opened my bag. I guess I'm just not used to trusting people I don't know. Maybe I've been awfully rude. Excuse me, please, will you, Mrs. Latham?"

It was wonderful. It was also all as plain as day. There was something in her bag that told all about Viola Kersey. I could have read it, and known, and never needed to ask. My asking was proof I hadn't opened the bag, and proof I didn't know. So Molly could afford to relax, then, accepting my statement, and to apologize so prettily for doubting my word. It was sweet . . . but I wasn't amused. I even wished devoutly that I *had* opened it.

"What's it all about, Molly?" I asked again. "Why don't you like Viola Van Zant?"

She looked at me calmly, as blankly innocent as a two-month-old blue-eyed spaniel.

"Viola Van Zant? Do you mean Mrs. Kersey? The woman with Eustace tonight?"

I said that was who I meant. The very same Mrs. Viola Van Zant Kersey who was with Eustace Sype in the cocktail lounge at the Casa del Flores where we and they had had dinner.

"I'm sure I have no idea, Mrs. Latham," she said politely. "I don't know what you're talking about. I've never seen Mrs. Kersey before, as far as I can remember. I only had a quick look at her, but I thought she was a horribly overdressed old hag, didn't you? I was surprised at Eustace having her out in public. He usually has people like that at his own house with the shades pulled down. But I'll find out, if you really want to know."

I was amused, then. I couldn't help but be. If I hadn't been, I would have had a vigorous impulse to turn the little wretch over my knee. I had one any way. Still, with everything, she was about the cutest and most engaging child I'd ever seen. I could understand better why Bill and Sheep thought she—and they—really had something.

I smiled at her. "Who else besides you wants Mrs. Kersey to leave the hotel by tomorrow noon, Molly?"

That struck a spark off, but nothing caught on fire. She was in control of herself. The play-acting was very nice.

"I must be stupid, Mrs. Latham," she said sweetly, "but I can't imagine what any of this is about. You *can't* think I *meant* what I said this afternoon. The boys wanted me to put on an act for you, so I did. I thought I might as well make it good while I was at it, and then carry it on by pretending I didn't know it was you when Bill introduced me. I must have been better than I thought I was, if you took it seriously."

She smiled at me. "And I'd better go. I'm awfully sorry if I've upset you."

She went gracefully across to the door and put her hand on the knob.

"And Mrs. Latham," she said, "you needn't worry about Bill. I know how mothers are. I'm not going to marry him. Or Sheep either. There's no love stuff. That's part of the deal. Bill and Sheep explained that to me the first thing. And Mother and Dad explained it to them too. They wouldn't have let me come if it hadn't been all down straight. So you don't have to worry. They're not in love with me and I'm not in love with them."

She opened the door a little, smiling sweetly at me.

"I thought I'd better explain in case you'd got the wrong idea—and I knew you would get it. That's why I didn't want you to come out here, Mrs. Latham—that's why I burned the letter they wrote you, instead of mailing it like I was supposed to. Because I knew you wouldn't approve of me. I know I'm just a girl they picked up in a juke box joint. But my parents——"

A voice outside in the hall interrupted her. "Maid."

She looked around quickly and pulled the door open for the woman to come in.

"Good evening, madam. May I turn your bed down now?"

The maid was a middle-aged woman with greying hair and a stern no-nonsense face. As I nodded, she turned to Molly.

"You've got a call for seven-thirty under your door, Miss McShane. And Bill's looking all over for you. You'd better get some sleep tonight if you've got to be up early."

Miss McShane seemed to me to be a little dashed at being interrupted in her best scene. I supposed the maid had seen too much of Hollywood in undress to be impressed by any raw recruit.

"I'm going, Rose. Right away. I really am."

She put her sweet society air back on for an instant, smiling at me, and then was gone in a flash. Unlike Mrs. Kersey, she wasn't afraid of what she looked like when she ran. And I was a little sorry myself that the woman had interrupted her. I hadn't had a chance to tell her about Mrs. Kersey's profound interest in her career, for one thing. But there would no doubt be another day.

"These girls," the maid said. "They don't think at night what they're going to look like in the morning. Some of them, anyway. Even the stars. You'd think they'd have learned."

She took the cover off the day bed, folded it up and brought a pair of pillows from the closet.

"If you hear anyone walking outside, don't be alarmed, madam," she said. She apparently held no very high idea of the whole place and seemed glad to talk to an outlander. "The night watchman makes his rounds every hour. It's to keep these crazy girls from disturbing the guests. They hide in the shrubbery and try to follow the male stars to their rooms. We're always having trouble with them. They drive some of the stars wild. Or like that girl up there now. They get her a taxi, and she's back at the bar. Nobody knows where she is now. The taxi comes, but it won't wait all night. But they'll find her. Is that all tonight, madam? I'll bring your wastebasket right back."

CHAPTER EIGHT

THAT WAS HOW I heard someone walking on tiptoe on the tiled floor of the hall between my room and the room of the man Bill had called "You Know Who," when he'd been out there earlier, irately demanding his solid, grated and juiced vegetables. I'd started into the bathroom to get my dressing gown, and mildly curious about people on tiptoe, I glanced around at the long mirror on the door in the middle of my inside wall. I saw a plump white hand raised to tap discreetly on the gentleman's door. It was Viola Kersey. She'd changed into a pair of lounging pajamas, of a warm smoky grey, no doubt an excellent color for discreet nocturnal wanderings. Mrs. Kersey rapped on the door with her left hand and turned the knob with her right. The door was unlocked. The next instant she had it open and her head inside, followed at once by the rest of her. The black frosted oak door was all that was left in the mirror.

Before I could turn to go about my own affairs, the maid appeared. She was coming back with the empty wastebasket in her hand, her head turned toward the door across the hall. As she came in she had the same look of dour disgust she'd had before, no more and no less. I dare say she was used to that sort of thing too. She put my wastebasket down by the table.

"Is there anything else, madam?"

"No, thanks," I said.

She started out. At the door she turned.

"I saw Sheep. He said if you weren't tired he'd come back and talk to you. Sheep's a fine boy. So is Bill. Everybody likes them. They're a lot better than some we get here. The guests, I mean. Not the help. The help's all nice."

I gathered she knew Bill was my son, though the watchdog look on her lined face wasn't changed.

As she went out she glanced at the door across the hall again. She was probably a good person, I thought—or not, depending on one's point of view—to have as night maid at a sprawling garden hotel.

I could hear Sheep outside—"Hi, Rose, about through this end?" —and the maid say, "31-B's the last. The lady says it's . . ." Her voice trailed off as Sheep got to where she was, and I waited so long, then, for Sheep that I'd about decided he wasn't coming when I heard him say, "Okay, good night, Rose," and heard his feet scrape the tiles as he came to my door.

"Well, what do you think of our dream boat, Mrs. Latham?"

He'd taken off his white coat and put on a plaid sport jacket that would have wrecked a train—a screaming medley of green, yellow and red. His black tie was gone with none to take its place, and his collar was opened down his lean sunburned throat.

"Gee, what a night." He sank down in my lounge chair and stretched his legs out. "I sure hope I never have to do this for a living. What do you think of our Miss Molly McShane?"

"She's terrific," I said.

"No fooling. Isn't she cute?"

"She really is. Awful cute."

"Oh, by the way." He leaned over and reached in his pocket. "Here's your lunch check. $1.75. Want to sign it?"

He picked up a pencil from the table and handed it to me with the check.

"I see she gave it back to you," I said, signing it for him. I could also see she hadn't told him anything about it. He reddened and gave me a dismayed sort of look before he relaxed and grinned.

"How did you know? Gee, you weren't supposed to see it. She was over at the pool with some guys, so I had to slip it to her on the quiet."

"So I gathered," I said. "And where's my son? I'd like to see him."

"Oh, there's some gal up there thinks she wants a taxi," he said. "They've got one for her, and Bill's trying to help the fellows find her. She's had a couple too many, is all." He pushed it aside as a familiar occurrence and furthermore one quite inconsequential in view of more pressing business at hand. "Anyway, we figured *I'd* better talk to you. You see, we're sort of in a real jam, Mrs. Latham, and we thought maybe we could get you to help us out of it."

It was a different Sheep from the infectiously grinning and debonair young man in the white coat earlier in the evening. The fan-shaped smile wrinkles at the corners of his direct and serious blue eyes were smoothed out. I thought he was a tough-minded young man, and one you'd think twice about crossing if he happened to get sore at something.

"You see, it's like this, Mrs. Latham. And don't start screaming until you hear it all." He gave me an ironic grin and leaned forward. "It's like this. There are a lot of angles we never thought about. I guess it was because our hearts were pure, or something. For instance: it sure never occurred to us that driving Molly up here from Texas was going to land us with a charge of transporting a minor. Gosh, we just figured it was a way to save train fare. It was all on the up and up—but we don't want some screwball to drag us into court to make us prove it. It would make mighty cute headlines for a gossip column, but it wouldn't help Molly."

"I can see that," I said.

"So . . . what we want you to do is stay here, and establish legal guardianship over Molly——"

"Stop!" I said. "Stop right there." I would have said it sooner if I could have caught my breath quicker. "*Me?* Establish legal guardian-ship over Molly McShane? Good heavens, Sheep!"

He was nodding earnestly. He really meant it.

"Look," I said, a little more calmly. "The answer is No. Abso-lutely No. I'd just as soon take over the tiger cage in the Zoo. You and Bill can study very nicely in jail, and I'll go home——"

"She's sweet, Mrs. Latham," Sheep said gently. "She's one of the sweetest kids you've seen. I mean really. You don't know her."

The lean freckled face that had been so tough a minute before had changed almost comically.

"Are you in love with this girl?" I asked.

His face got red. He ran his fingers through his curly ginger-colored hair.

"That stuff's out, Mrs. Latham. We all agreed on that. That'd wreck everything. You must have been listening to Lucille Gannon. That's all she thinks about. No, it's nothing like that, Mrs. Latham. This is a straight deal."

I imagine he thought it was the truth he was telling. He looked and sounded to me very much like a young man in love, aware or unaware of it as he might be. And Lucille Gannon apparently thought so too, and she'd had a lot more experience than either Bill or Sheep Clarke . . . pain though they appeared to agree she was.

"We're both nuts about her, of course," Sheep added hastily. "I don't mean to say we aren't. That's what makes it sort of tough deciding . . ."

"Deciding what?" I asked, when he trailed off unhappily and began to fish around in his pocket for a lighter.

"Well, you see, if we can't get you to help us, there's only one other way we can figure. That's to marry her."

I stared at him.

"Sure. Then it would all be straightened out."

"Which one of you does she propose to marry?" I asked, as calmly as I could.

"Oh, it doesn't matter to her. It'd just be a deal, you see. Till she's twenty-one. Then we'd call it quits. But——"

He paused again.

"But what?"

"Why, we can't make up our minds which of us ought to . . . I mean which one . . ."

"Wants to sacrifice himself," I suggested. I thought I'd better help him out.

He reddened, but he grinned this time. "I guess so." He fished around and got his lighter. "Bill's got the most dough, but I've got a couple of sisters. I know more about girls than Bill does."

"I think you're crazy," I said. "All three of you—but you and Bill are crazier than Molly. And now you seem to me to be headed for real trouble."

"We hoped you'd——"

"Listen, Sheep," I said. "Molly has parents. Or has she?"

"Oh, sure."

"All right. They're her legal guardians. She doesn't——"

He shook his head. "That's the trouble, Mrs. Latham. They're in a kind of funny position. They're okay—I don't mean they aren't—but . . . well, they're just ordinary people. They——"

"Most parents are."

"I know. But—these people are afraid they'd handicap her. They're crazy about her, and terribly proud of her. But they're afraid they'd hurt her. Her father doesn't speak very good English, and her mother wants to . . . well, she wants to keep in the background. It's not that they think she'd be ashamed of them, if you see what I mean."

"I'm afraid I don't, Sheep," I said. "Aristocratic parents have never been a Hollywood must that I've ever heard of."

"This is different," he said stubbornly. "And don't get our little girl wrong. She thinks they're swell. But she sees the point . . . about the McShanes, I mean. And this other dame—she hates her guts."

"Would you mind telling me why, Sheep? Bill says she doesn't even know the woman's name . . . and she certainly doesn't know what she looks like."

It occurred to me that having said so much I might as well go on.

"In fact, I don't really think your little girl is being very frank with you two guys. And if she hasn't told you whatever it is she knows about Mrs. Viola Van Zant Kersey in 31-B I know she isn't."

He shook his head. "Why should she be, Mrs. Latham?" he said gently. "We don't own her. If there's something she doesn't want to tell us, why the hell can't she keep it to herself if she wants to? If she's got something to hide, that's her business. And it's nothing wrong, Mrs. Latham. We know her—she's okay. If she's in trouble, we're with her. We're not going to kick her overboard just because somebody's trying to louse up the deal."

I'd been telling myself all evening that I had to keep my mouth shut. It was that kind of a spot I was in. I had to watch my step. It was hard to make any kind of suggestion at all without giving them the impression that I was definitely against their little dream boat.

"I'm sorry," I said. "All I meant was that this whole thing is crazy. You and Bill are worried about 'this dame.' You don't know who she is. I'll bet you a hundred dollars she's Viola Van Zant Kersey. That's all I mean. I think Molly knows it's Mrs. Kersey. If you know what else it's about, I don't. But I should have told Molly, and I'll tell you, that Mrs. Kersey says she's very much interested in the three of you and wants to help you out. What's money for, Mrs. Kersey says, if you can't use it for others? She also says she knew Molly's mother and she was a bad and wicked woman——"

"That is . . . false," Sheep said calmly. "In fact it's a damned lie. We know Molly's mother. She's worked like a hound to get the kid some place. She'd kill herself if she thought it would do the baby any good. I tell you, we know. We've seen them both—her mother and her father. They're fine. It's just that they're scared of this racket the kid's in, this dog-eat-dog fight. They know you can't go in with any kind of a strike against you. That's all that worries them. That's why we wanted you to take over, Mrs. Latham. We asked Lucille Gannon, but she hit the ceiling."

"Why don't you think of Mrs. Kersey next?" I suggested peaceably. "She says she wants to help you."

"No thanks," he said shortly. "She can suck up to Gee Gee Gannon all she wants to, and let her. She's not playing in our game."

I looked at him. "Gee Gee Gannon? Lucille's husband? He's in Palm Springs——"

"He's right straight across the hall from you, Mrs. Latham," Sheep said. "Lucille's in Palm Springs. Gee Gee's in the next room. Also, your Viola Van Zant's in there with him."

"Oh," I said.

CHAPTER NINE

I was a little like Molly, it seemed. Here was someone whose name I knew and that was all. I'd had no idea what Lucille Gannon's husband looked like. I tried to think of the man Lucille had met one day, fallen in love with and rushed to Las Vegas and married six weeks later, all in such a passionate whirlwind that her second husband hardly knew what had happened. Her Dream Prince, Gee Gee was then, and of course still might be, though I'd always thought of a Dream Prince as having more hair and less avoirdupois.

"He's supposed to be holed in working on a script," Sheep said. "No phone calls, no visitors. He's sure been sweating it out today. If the picture hits the audience the way it has him, they'll all wake up in the N. P. ward. Lucille ought to come and take him home and call the doctor. I bet I've taken him ten tubs of ice since one o'clock."

He tossed his cigarette into the fireplace.

"This is off the record. Nobody's supposed to know he's here. He's registered as George Smith. That's part of the clap-trap of being local Big Brass."

He grinned at me. "It would break Georgie's heart if nobody tried to get him, so his secretary calls up every twenty minutes and leaves a message under a different name. But Georgie's a nice guy, Mrs. Latham. It's just the pattern. He's okay. So keep it dark—and don't speak to him if you run into him, or I'd lose my job . . . for two days. And think it over, will you, Mrs. Latham. You know what they say . . . time is of the essence."

I looked at him. I had no idea whether he knew or didn't know, or believed or didn't believe, that Mrs. Viola Van Zant Kersey was their enemy, or if so, for what reason she was dangerous to Molly McShane. But one thing I did know, and that was that there wasn't any half-way house for Sheep. He was for Molly, and it didn't make any difference what Molly did. He was for her, and anyone against her was against Sheep Clarke. And he didn't look like the sort that would care much about the cost.

"Nobody's going to get their hooks in our girl, Mrs. Latham," he said evenly. "I'll see them in hell first."

It was the second time that day that I'd heard so. Molly had said it in the white heat of passionate fury. Sheep was quiet, but I thought he meant it.

"I'll see you in the morning," I said. "Tell Bill to go home and go to bed. I'll see him tomorrow, too."

"Good night, Mrs. Latham."

I closed the door behind him, with a glance at Gee Gee Gannon's door across the hall, and went over to the window to let in a little fresh air. I was pretty much disturbed. It seemed to me there was trouble ahead. I could smell it the way a sleeping dog can smell a pound of hamburger when the butcher boy opens the kitchen door. I pulled open the french window.

When the voice out of the darkness said, "Hello, there," I must have jumped a foot. There was someone on my patio. Then I realized who it was. It didn't take any imagination, from the sound of the voice, to do it, either. I pushed the curtain aside, and in the long yellow panel of light it let out into the night I saw the girl, huddled in a fur coat, reclining on the blue chaise longue. She pulled herself up, blinking into the sudden light.

"Did you give that girl her bag? I just wanted to know if you gave it to her."

Her voice was blurred and fuzzy.

"Yes, I did," I said.

"That's all I wanted to know. I've been looking all over for you, but you had company when I found you, so I just waited. I told you, didn't I? Didn't I tell you some screwy dame would figure we swiped it? Didn't I tell you?"

"Yes, you did," I said. "You did indeed. So now why don't you go home?"

"That's what I'm going to do. That's what I was going to do before. But I just wanted you to see I was right. Remember what I said to you? I said, some screwy dame's going to start yelling we lifted the crown jewels. Wasn't that just what I said? The very ee-zact words? And wasn't I right? You bet I was right. I know these dames down here."

She got up, balancing herself carefully against the wrought-iron table.

"Now I'm going home. Tomorrow I'm going *clear* home. Back to Seattle, Washington. Do you know where Seattle, Washington is?"

"Yes, I know," I said.

"Well, that's where I came from, and that's where I'm going back to. I can get a job there. I can get a job anywhere. I got a job here, but I don't like it. I'm going back to Seattle, Washington. I don't know why I came here when I had a good job there in the first place. What did you come here for?"

"I don't know either," I said, and with a good deal of truth now that the point had risen.

I held the screen aside as she came through, blinking in the lighted room.

"That's just it. Nobody knows—nobody ever knows." She stifled a yawn. "I've been asleep. I feel better now. Not much better but some better. Now I'm going to get a taxi and go home. *You* call me a taxi. Will you do that?"

"Yes," I said. "I'll do that."

"Okay. Goodbye. And remember what I said about these dames around here. Remember? I said——"

"I know," I said. "I'll remember it. And you wait. I'll call a taxi, and then I'll walk out with you."

An indignant light came into her eyes. "You think I'm drunk. Well, I am. But I can walk. Nobody ever has to walk any place with me. I can walk by myself. I found you, didn't I? I didn't need any help to find you. And I can find my way back. You just call me a taxicab. That's all I want. I don't want anything else."

"All right," I said. "Goodbye."

She went out. I thought she was steady enough to make it, so I called the desk and ordered a cab for her.

I didn't know until ten minutes to one that she didn't make it. The night watchman found her. She was lying at the foot of the steps that led down to Mrs. Kersey's suite on the lower terrace. It was a long flight of steps, made of jagged stone. She looked pitifully young, but at peace, lying there under the light.

When I got out, having heard the voices and gathered something serious had happened, the first thing I saw was Viola Kersey, standing there in the half-dark, on the steps just below the top. I supposed she was just returning from Gee Gee Gannon's room across the hall from me. At any rate he hadn't come with her; she was alone, when I saw her, and standing there as if rigid. When I went up to her she was so absorbed, staring down at her feet, that she didn't see me coming.

Suddenly she bent down, and straightened quickly up again. She saw me then. It was light enough for me to see that her face was ashen, her eyes big blue hollows. She turned quickly toward me.

"She tripped," she whispered. "On a string. It was tied across——"

Mrs. Kersey stopped, staring silently at me for an instant.

"My God!" she whispered then. "It could have been me."

She started to go on, and stopped. But I saw what she was going to say, in the kind of pasty horror that crumpled her face. It not only could have been . . . it was meant for her. She knew it was.

Mrs. Kersey's eyes moved unconsciously to the sign on the rail at the top of the step. "Private Entrance—31-B Only." She raised her hand and rubbed it slowly across her flaccid chin. Mrs. Kersey was an enormously shaken woman.

"You'd better sit down," I said. I thought if she didn't she was going to topple over and go on down to the bottom anyway. "Sit down, and I'll get the policeman."

The word seemed to startle her, but she didn't at once try to stop me. It wasn't till I'd turned and got down three steps toward the grim concentrated group on the terrace below.

"Oh, Mrs. Latham . . ."

I turned back quickly.

"Oh, my dear, how stupid of me!"

The voice was phoney. I'd known that from the sound of the "Oh, Mrs. Latham."

"Look, my dear. It wasn't a string at all. It was just this old vine, that looked like a string. Oh, wouldn't that have been terrible?"

The vine she had hold of came over the top of the rail, not underneath it on the step where she'd been staring when I first saw her. I looked down there. No string was in sight, there or in her hands.

"Just think how dreadful a mistake that would have been. It would have looked as if I was afraid somebody was laying a trap for me! Because this is my stairway. It would have been like casting perfectly horrible suspicion on . . . on somebody, wouldn't it?"

She glanced at me more sharply as I didn't say anything.

"You understand there wasn't any string, Mrs. Latham," she said.

"You didn't *see* a string, did you? I said there was one and I was wrong. Because there isn't any string, Mrs. Latham."

There was a string. She knew it, and she knew I knew it. She'd been able to untie it and she'd probably stuffed it in her lavish bosom the instant I'd turned my back to go down and get the policeman.

"I can't imagine what I was thinking of." She said that with an airy laugh. "I have no enemies. I haven't an enemy in the world."

Her voice was as light as her laughter, but she still had me fixed with an eye that had no lightness or laughter in it.

"You don't believe me, Mrs. Latham. I can see you don't. But surely you don't think there's anyone who would want to do that to me?"

She nodded down at the crumpled heap at the foot of the jagged stone steps. One of the men had moved. The lights picked out a small moving trickle of blood on the girl's forehead.

"—Or do you, Mrs. Latham?" she said softly. "I'm quite sure you don't. But we don't want any misunderstanding about it. I'll tell the policeman myself.—Oh, Captain!"

She turned back to me. "It isn't as if you'd actually seen a string, is it? It's so easy to be mistaken when you're all upset.—Captain . . . this vine . . ."

She held it out to the young police officer. But it was me she was looking at. She was looking at me and smiling.

That was how, instead of concealing the fact that the girl who wanted to go back to Seattle, Washington, had been murdered, Mrs. Kersey succeeded in suggesting it. She could have taken the gift the Fates had handed her and kept still about it. Instead, she pressed them just one step too far. Up to that point the Los Angeles County Police had taken it for granted that death was accidental. It seems to have been Viola Kersey's signal weakness. She never knew when to let well enough alone.

CHAPTER TEN

MRS. VIOLA KERSEY was the shattered little woman helplessly appeal-ing to the great big policeman, and making a mean suspicious harpy out of me . . . if indeed not actually an object of suspicion.

"This lady won't believe me, Captain." She held the trailing piece of honeysuckle vine out in her fluttering white hands. "I thought this was a green cord and maybe that poor girl tripped on it. I didn't mean to say anybody put it here on purpose, but that's what she seems to think I meant." She motioned at me. "It does look like a green cord, doesn't it? And lying on the step it looked so much like one . . . It must have been the awful shock of seeing that poor girl down there. I must have been so shocked I was hysterical."

She'd said "string," not "green cord," and she must have had cat's eyes or a flashlight to see it lying in the shadow of the stone step. And she wasn't so shocked or hysterical that she hadn't had presence of mind enough to slip the vine under the rail from where it had been over it, and strip off the leaves so that it did in fact look like a green cord. In the brief space of time my back had been turned she'd done some fast thinking and fast acting. What it added up to, however, was not what Mrs. Kersey wanted.

Moreover the young police officer was not a captain. He was a uniformed sergeant in charge of the radio patrol car cruising the area, who'd picked up the call relayed from the Santa Monica and Fairfax Substation of the Sheriff's Office of Los Angeles County, which had jurisdiction. But he was nobody's fool, and Mrs. Kersey was neither young enough, nor motherly enough, nor frail enough, for any moist-eyed fluttering helplessness to have too much effect on him.

He took the vine out of her hand and looked at it—and her—a little oddly. He ran his flashlight along it.

"The leaves have been stripped off," he said soberly. "You can see where it's peeled."

He swept his light over the high shrubbery at the side of the steps. A few leaves thrown over the rail had caught on it.

"Looks like you got something, lady. Looked like accidental death. They said at the office she was roaming around stewed to the gills."

He turned and called down the steps to the man by the girl's body.

"Phil—hold everything. I'm going to call the Chief. Just leave things alone."

If he hadn't been looking at Phil and had been looking at Viola Kersey he would have been a surprised young man. There was a look of startled dismay on her face as she realized what she'd done. And she didn't like it. For one instant the appealing little woman looked for all the world like the household variety of virago who's sweet as all get out as long as guests are present and ready to snatch the family bald-headed as soon as the door is closed. Mrs. Kersey had been too smart. If she'd left the trailing vine on top of the rail, or merely left the leaves on it, there would have been no question about her story. But she'd been desperately anxious, for some reason, to convince me that I hadn't heard her, and her efficiency had backfired in a big way.

I could hear her breath coming in angry little jerks, and the glance she darted me was lethal. When the young sergeant turned back she'd caught hold of herself. It was not a very pleasant self. I was a little appalled that Molly McShane could ever have thought that here was a woman she could frighten off with a verbal blistering or the rock and telephone technique. It only proved what I already knew. Molly McShane was as ignorant of the nature as of the appearance of what she was up against.

Mrs. Kersey started to shiver. "Oh, Captain, I'm so cold . . . I wonder if I could get my coat? I'm freezing . . ."

It was cold, but not that cold, and only an aspen leaf or somebody with an ague could have reacted so violently.

"Sure," the sergeant said. "You might as well wait in your room till we see what the Chief wants. Where are you going?"

Mrs. Kersey had started, at a pretty fast clip, down the stairs, not back the way she'd come.

"To my room. That's my room down there. I was just coming back to it."

She drew herself up, half in hurt surprise and half in honest indignation. "And you have no right to keep me here freezing to death, young man. I had nothing to do with that girl down there. I never saw her but once in my life, and that was after dinner when she was coming out of the Powder Room in front of Mrs. Latham there. If you want information you'd better get it from her. It looks to me as if the girl must have been coming from somebody's room, and hers is right there. You'd better ask her what she knows about it."

Mrs. Kersey was merely playing for time and privacy. I'm sure she hadn't the foggiest idea that there was any truth in what she was saying, or any possible consequences in it for herself. It was hardly even a shot in the dark, the merest distracting of attention from herself until she could get rid of the length of twine that I was sure she had on her. Of course it's too late now, but someone, at some point, should have taught Viola Kersey the basic and canonical truth of leaving well enough alone. It was unfortunate that no one ever had. And the irony of it was that she seemed enormously pleased with herself. For the second time she looked at me and smiled, like a spoiled brat sticking out its tongue.

I had to take it . . . and I was very glad I hadn't already told the simplified form of my story, which was what I'd been planning to do when the time came. The small harmless gaps in it, if the girl had only fallen down the stairs, would have looked like canyons full of twisting rattlesnakes the minute murder was suggested, as it now was. It was unimportant that it was accidental murder, and that if any victim had been intended it was the occupant of 31-B, now picking her way down the steps, very cautiously in case a reserve string had been set up and had been overlooked by all.

"What's this about, ma'am?"

The sergeant was slightly bewildered but on the alert, and his manner toward me had suffered a change. He was polite, and cool.

"I'll be very happy to tell you all I know," I said. "Which isn't much. The girl was in my room. I don't know her at all. Do you want me to make a statement now, or do I wait till somebody from Homicide gets here?"

He didn't know he was dealing with an old and experienced hand, who'd been around murder so often, thanks to the company she kept in the Janus-faced person of Colonel Primrose and Sergeant Buck, that the kindest thing said about her was "Where there's so much smoke there must be some fire," and the least kind but most frequent that she was a Typhoid Mary, murder and mayhem always with her. And—like Mrs. Kersey—I needed time, even if I had to stand on my constitutional rights to get it.

I also needed Colonel Primrose and Sergeant Buck. I'd have called the Colonel then and there, except that the young officer decided to use my phone to call his Chief. The guarded way he talked over the phone made it evident he thought I was being deliberately evasive, which was perfectly correct, I suppose—though I didn't want to evade the issue as much as I wanted to sort out its various meanings and complications before we were all tied up in so many

knots we could never undo them. What I should have liked to do
was see Molly McShane. But that was out of the question. Any belief
I had that it might be possible was dissolved when the police sergeant
said a final "Okay, sir," and put down the phone.

"I guess you'd better stay here, ma'am, until the Chief gets out.
I've got to see who I can round up. You'd just have to give your
statement over again."

His self-confidence seemed a little shaken, and I imagined it had
been pointed out to him over the phone that he was in an exclusive
hotel and he'd better be careful about shouting murder until he was
sure murder was what it was.

I closed the door after him. In the next room Mrs. Ansell, the
writer, was coughing again. Across the hall there was total silence.
If Gee Gee Gannon had any curiosity about what was going on
outside his back windows, or any interest in what his nocturnal lady
guest had barged out into, he was not showing it. Only once did I
think I heard a stealthy footstep out in the hall, but I couldn't be
sure. I should have thought just natural curiosity would have made
him wonder what was going on. Unless he was unconscious, he
couldn't have helped knowing something was.

Mrs. Ansell's phone rang once. I could hear it, and her, so plainly
that they might have been in my own room.

"A blonde with her neck broken! Good Lord! Look, darling—it
isn't Miss Lana Turner by any chance, is it?" Then she laughed.
"No, I certainly don't wish her any bad luck, but I'm sitting around
waiting to see her. No, dear—I don't know anything about what's
going on outside. No, not yet. I was supposed to see her today but
according to the columnists she's in Palm Springs—with Frankie and
some people. I'm bored—there could be a general massacre and it
wouldn't interest me. No, I haven't seen anything . . . oh, except
some gal who was on my patio early this evening. She said she was
hunting some dame who'd stolen her bag, or something. She was
too far gone to make much sense, so if she'd fallen down the steps
she'd have collapsed in a nice relaxed heap. Otherwise, darling, I've
been in solitary. Tell me all about it in the morning. Goodbye."

Whether a writer saw Miss Lana Turner or not didn't interest
me, but I was vitally and personally interested in what she'd had to
say about the girl on the patio. If she told the police the girl had said
she was hunting some dame who'd stolen her bag, any hope of

keeping the bag out of it was dim. How dim, I found out not too many minutes later. And the police didn't hear it from Mrs. Ansell. It was from my own flesh and blood, former Navy Air Force Reserve Lieutenant William A. Latham, blissfully unconscious of the fact that he was giving his little dream boat and Sheep's a terrific shove out into the high seas with a typhoon raging toward her, a frail and tiny craft.

Captain Crawford from the Sheriff's Office was a quiet, soft-spoken man. I may be wrong, but all of them seemed a little grateful that it wasn't another one of the ghastly werewolf cycle the City and County police were just beginning to be deluged with, to the drooling delight and zooming circulation of a couple of the local newspapers. At least the girl wasn't in an open field butchered with maniacal frenzy. She was asleep and at peace, with none of the horror and anguish and abnormality that made a Hollywood writer I know suggest, after the sixth one in fewer months, that it all looked like a macabre publicity stunt.

Captain Crawford didn't like the idea of any kind of murder, but he went at it patiently and honestly.

An officer came for me, and I went with him to the manager's office where Captain Crawford was talking to the people they'd rounded up. The night watchman was there, and Rose, the night maid. Mrs. Kersey was there, and a bellboy named Nat. And Bill Latham and Sheep Clarke. I looked at them with complete surprise. I thought they'd gone home a long time ago. My surprise turned to real dismay as I heard Bill Latham talking.

"All I was trying to do was help Nat and Morry." He nodded at the night watchman, who was sitting with his time clock strung about his neck, a long envelope clutched tightly in his hands, looking about as miserable a little man as I've ever seen. He had beads of perspiration on his forehead that he kept wiping off with the back of his hand, which he then wiped off on the seat of his worn pants. He looked like some unobtrusive little mole who'd taken to night watching to avoid the sunshine, and was just as uncomfortable in the bright artificial light of the manager's office.

"She'd call a taxi, and then disappear. They won't wait out here more than five or ten minutes. I said I'd take her home in my jalopy. She wouldn't go till she'd seen some woman she'd talked to. It was about somebody's pocketbook. She found it in the telephone booth and gave it to this woman. The dame that owned it was making a row—said this girl had lifted it and stolen the jewels in it."

My heart sank. But not the police stenographer's. He wrote with renewed energy.

"She wanted to prove she hadn't stolen them, so she had to find this woman. Or that's what she thought. She was pretty tight. We tried to get her in the car, but she ducked back in the grounds. And that's the last we saw of her. We told Morry and Rose to keep an eye out, but they didn't find her, did you, Morry? Did you, Rose? And you didn't see her, did you, Sheep?"

Neither Rose nor Sheep had seen her after she left the central patio. Captain Crawford turned to the night watchman. He was trying to get a paper out of the envelope he was clutching.

"I'm U. S. A. citizen, see?"

He handed his passport to freedom over, keeping his hand out. "That's fine, Mr. Shavin. You're Lithuanian?"

"American. Not Lithuanian. See—U. S. A. citizen."

"That's right, Mr. Shavin." Captain Crawford handed his paper back to him. "Put it in your pocket, and let's hear about tonight."

It was hard going for the stenographer. The night watchman was voluble, now that he'd put himself on a proper footing in the sight of constituted police authority. He had tried to find the girl and almost mistaken another woman for her. It was the kind of job to drive anybody crazy, with women always hanging around the parking area trying to waylay the stars, and getting in the grounds to find their rooms. It was enough to drive the saints crazy, trying to know who to stop and who to let alone. He would have stopped the woman he saw and got into a lot of trouble, most likely, if she hadn't gone out the end gate and got in her own car just in time. He mopped his forehead with a blue cotton handkerchief. People didn't like to be questioned. He'd got into a lot of trouble many times, trying to do his duty. Once he had stopped a lady star at three o'clock in the morning, trying to get out the end gate just the same way.

He locked the end gate at half-past eleven every night, and he was not allowed to let people out that way. The lady star was visiting her husband, and the papers got hold of it, because they were getting publicity for her new picture about the two of them being separated. There was a lot of trouble. The things he could tell them! He could tell them all night about the crazy troubles he'd had. And it sounded as if he was going to, until Captain Crawford stopped him.

"When did you go down the steps to 31-B the last time, Shavin?"

It was twenty-five minutes past ten, Morry Shavin said, except that he went up them, not down. He was just coming to the top of the steps when he saw Mr. Eustace Sype coming out of the hall between 101 and 102. He waited there for him, walked to his car with him, came back and finished his round, looking for the girl. On his eleven o'clock round he went along the flagstone path in front of my cottage around to the patios in the rear, then down the steps by Mrs. Ansell's to the end gate, which he then locked at eleven-thirty. He went back by the path in front of 31-B. It was at twelve twenty-five that he came up the steps again, and that time he didn't come up, because he found the girl at the bottom. He didn't realize at first that she was dead. Hotels don't like scandal. He had tried to move the girl and discovered she was dead. He got the assistant manager up, and the police were called.

"You didn't notice the vine across the steps then?" Captain Crawford asked.

Shavin shook his head positively. He had run up the steps to get the assistant manager, both of them had come down again, neither had noticed any vine. They were used to vines and they were both excited. Maybe there was a vine, maybe there was not.

"Now, the woman who owned these jewels . . ."

"There weren't any jewels, Captain Crawford," I put in.

It seemed to me it was time to stop this nonsense or I'd find myself at the end of their blind alley accused of receiving stolen goods.

"That was just a joke. The girl picked the bag up in the telephone booth and gave it to me to return to the owner because she was going. It belonged to Molly McShane, and I gave it back to her."

"Then what was all this excitement about jewels——" Captain Crawford began.

"It was just the state the girl was in," I said. "I doubt if she was a very reliable reporter. I'm sure Miss McShane can tell you what happened. All I know is the girl was on my patio while you were in the room, Sheep. I'm not very clear about the time, but it must have been almost eleven when she left my room, or a little after that."

Captain Crawford was examining his notes. Actually, I thought, he was quietly absorbing the heightened vibrations set up by just the mention of Molly McShane's name. He must have been completely insentient, as well as deaf, dumb and blind, not to be aware of them, or the startled surprise on Bill's face, or the quick glance he and Sheep exchanged. And Viola Kersey was even more startled. I think she was realizing fully that, instead of jumping the pond, she'd landed plop in the middle of it, and under circumstances that made it impolitic to call for help. The maid and the night watchman were completely impassive—too familiar, I supposed, with the general whoopdedoo of their less stable customers to be surprised at anything.

"Where is this Miss McShane?" Captain Crawford inquired, of no one in particular.

"She's gone to bed," the maid said abruptly. "She has a seven-thirty call. Do you want me to get her? She needs her sleep."

"In the morning will do," Captain Crawford said. "It'll do for all of you if you'll be here around ten-thirty. By that time we ought to be able to find out who this girl was, and who she was seeing here at the hotel."

It seemed to me an abrupt and surprising dismissal. Mrs. Kersey had not been questioned at all, as far as I knew. She had the appearance of someone with a story all made up to tell and no one to tell it to. But perhaps it was just intended to be told to the maid, Rose, who'd started off immediately.

"Maid," she said. "You didn't leave me enough hand towels. Will you bring some, and bring me a pitcher of ice cubes. I'd like some left in my room every night."

She turned to me. "Are you coming, Mrs. Latham?"

"I'd like to speak to Mrs. Latham a minute," Captain Crawford said. "The rest of you can go along." He looked at Bill and Sheep, waiting by the door. "You two go home. Be sure and be here in the morning. And you too, Dad."

"Okay, okay." Mr. Shavin went out with Bill and Sheep. They walked down to the entrance gate, leaving the bellboy, Nat, to escort Mrs. Kersey to her room.

"That your son, Mrs. Latham?" Captain Crawford inquired pleasantly, nodding after them.

I said yes.

"And the other one? He's a friend of your son's?"

I said yes again. "They were in the War together. Navy fliers."

"And they're waiters here now?"

"They're in school," I said. "They're waiters on the side."

"I like to see boys with some git up and git to them," he said. "Now this McShane girl. She a friend of theirs?"

I nodded.

"From all I hear, I guess they think quite a lot of her?"

It seemed to me it was a form of dialectic leading to only one point. He could have skipped it all and got there quicker.

"They'd do about anything for her, I guess, wouldn't they?"

"They wouldn't tie a string or a vine over a step for somebody to trip on for her, if that's what you mean," I said.

Captain Crawford smiled benignly.

"That string business is interesting, isn't it, Mrs. Latham? We can't tell tonight, but it looks as if whoever tied a string, or a vine, there— if they did—must have had somebody in mind. They'd be going down the steps. That lets out old Shavin—he'd be coming up. Looks like this Mrs. Kersey would be the one most likely to be going down them, doesn't it? That is, if they knew she was out of her room. Now if they didn't, it might be somebody they figured was going down to visit her. Or it could be just somebody *she* figured would be going down there while she was away."

I was a little startled at that, for an instant.

"But that isn't likely," I said. "The maid went down after Mrs. Kersey came up. If Mrs. Kersey did it, it would mean she had to go out of the room she was visiting, tie the string there and come back. It seems highly involved, to me."

"I didn't say it was the case," Captain Crawford said blandly. "You just have to consider all angles. What was in Miss McShane's bag, Mrs. Latham?"

The surprise technique was altogether too simple just then. I shook my head.

"What do you know about Mrs. Kersey?"

"Nothing at all. I never saw her before this evening at dinner."

"Now, that's *interesting*. I would have taken my oath on it when you two were sitting here tonight that you knew her better than that, and you didn't much like her. That's just the idea I got when you came in the room. And I thought your son and Clarke didn't like her any better than you did. It's funny how you get ideas, isn't it?"

I agreed that it was.

"I'll just walk back your way with you, Mrs. Latham," he said. "I think maybe it would be a good idea for nobody to get too curious, or try any amateur detective stuff like you see in the movies—like those two boys, for instance, when they get to wishing they'd kept still about the bag. You never know what you might run into—it's so blessed dark around here at night."

We came to the steps. "You couldn't see a vine if it was tied to the other post under that step, could you, very well, now?" he asked, glancing down at it. "You sure couldn't. So good night, Mrs. Latham. Don't worry about that boy of yours. I'll see they go home, in case they had any ideas of hanging around. I suppose Viola Van Zant was before your time to go to the movies, wasn't she?"

"No, I remember her very well," I said. "We asked the waiter who she was tonight. I couldn't remember then, but she looked familiar."

"She made quite a name for herself in her day," he said. "A lot of people still around here didn't like her much, in those days. Jealousy, maybe. It's a funny business. I guess there's more jealousy concentrated in these ten square miles you're in now than any place there is. Well, I guess that's life, as they say."

He was looking down at Mrs. Kersey's cottage. Every light was on, outside as well as in. It was a pool of brilliance in the surrounding darkness, but the silence of it gave it the false static quality a house has when it's been full of people who've all gone home.

"I guess she's more comfortable that way," Captain Crawford said. "I guess that's the main difference between people and animals. Animals feel safer in the dark. Or maybe she's just waiting for her hand towels and that pitcher of ice. My wife used to spend an hour every night putting ice on her face to keep it from sagging, but she gave up finally. I guess it was too much trouble. It sure made her a lot easier to live with. Well, good night, Mrs. Latham."

He looked around. Rose was plugging along the flagstone path toward us with towels and a pitcher. The ice cubes clinked angrily at every step, and as she came up we could see a dour gleam in her eye.

"Take it easy," Captain Crawford said. "Don't get riled up. You wouldn't expect the lady to use the same towel twice, would you?"

The maid looked at him impassively. "You can always tell them." There was a tinge of bitterness in her voice. "People that are really used to things don't go around making extra trouble for the help just to prove they are somebody."

We watched her go heavily down the steps and into 31-B.

"Hope she didn't throw it at her," Captain Crawford remarked. "Well, good night, Mrs. Latham."

I went on into my own room. In a moment Captain Crawford's footsteps grated on the tiled hall floor and I heard him knock on the door across from mine. I heard him say "Mr. Smith? Sorry to bother you."

He probably wasn't half as sorry, I thought, as "Mr. Smith." It must be hard at best to explain to the police why you're in a hotel under an assumed name. A dead girl on the doorstep, a middle-aged lady in grey pajamas going home at one o'clock, must add a certain element of hazard even if you're innocent as the whole company of angels. And that George Gannon, even if he had not appeared, was still awake was evident from the speed with which Captain Crawford's "Mr. Smith?" had followed his knock on the door. It had taken Mrs. Kersey longer than that to get in.

It's no doubt wrong to enjoy anyone else's discomfiture . . . and anyway, it wasn't George Gannon's that I found myself a little amused at as I went to bed. It was Lucille Gannon's. If she could regard Bill and Sheep's chaperonage of Molly McShane as moral dissolution, or, as Bill thought, her husband's professional interest in Molly as an intimate and personal one, she wasn't likely to take a kindly and optimistic view of the lady in grey pajamas visiting him at this time of night. The pleasure of hearing her try to explain it was something I looked forward to, rather, and I turned off my light in a more relaxed frame of mind than I would have done if I'd been thinking about Bill and Sheep and Molly McShane. I had to get up at last, however, and close my bathroom door. The glow of the lights from Mrs. Kersey's cottage came through the frosted window. There was no use waiting till she turned them off, because it was at length apparent she was going to leave them on all night. That more than anything else made it obvious that Mrs. Kersey was not very easy in her mind. It wouldn't have surprised me in the least to have been waked by a strangled scream from the lower terrace. But I wasn't—I was waked by a telephone bell vibrating through the wall.

It was in Mrs. Ansell's room next to mine. The abruptness of the early morning call set her coughing again. I looked at my clock. It was eight, and the sun was streaming in the patio windows. Mrs. Ansell was talking, to New York, I gathered. Her voice was almost as plain as if she were in the room with me.

"I know, dear. Of course it's my fault. But no matter how cordial a producer and director are, I can't write a story about their star if their star won't see me, can I? I mean, I can't afford to just sit around indefinitely . . . not when I have to pay four dollars and forty-three cents for a pitcher of orange juice, when there's a whole tree full of them outside my front door. Yes, I know, dear. It comes off my income tax. I could pay my income tax and buy a rototiller for the farm and be ahead in the long run. I *know* stars are spoiled lambs, darling, but I *work* for a living. Okay, I'll stick it a little longer."

Mrs. Ansell had put down the phone. At least I was getting a different sidelight on the glittering goldfish bowl that is Hollywood. I'd always thought publicity was the seed it fed on, but apparently some stars preferred to have a private life. I gathered Mrs. Ansell had felt the same way and was a very discouraged woman finding it not so. Then I heard her call "Come in. Oh, good morning, Sheep. How are you, and what's this I hear about a murder last night?"

"That's crazy."

The sound of Sheep Clarke's voice brought me suddenly back to the whole business of the night before. It had lost its reality somehow during the night. Captain Crawford's knocking at George Gannon's door had had the effect of removing it from the three people I was interested in . . . Bill and Sheep and Molly McShane. I'd forgotten that Sheep Clarke was a waiter and that when my breakfast came he'd be the one to bring it. The sound of his voice brought it sharply back.

"That's absolutely crazy. A gal around here had a skinful and took a header down those steps. It's too bad, but there's no use everybody starting to yell bloody murder. It was that dame down in 31-B. And you don't even have to yell—a whisper's enough to get it going all over the place. It's lousy with cops out there now."

"She can yell or whisper or anything else," Mrs. Ansell said. "All I wish is she'd turn her lights out at night. I'll have to get a bathroom shade if she doesn't. My door doesn't stay closed, and I kept waking up every ten minutes. She certainly entertains at odd hours. My next-door neighbor was down there at three."

"—*Mrs. Latham?*"

"No, the man in 101. He about scared the daylights out of me, stumbling down behind the patios. I wouldn't have heard him if the light hadn't kept me awake. And then Molly——"

"*Molly?*" Sheep's voice had been surprised at the thought that it was me. It was sharpened with anxiety now.

"Molly. At least I guess she'd been down there. She was halfway down the steps, at half-past four . . . crying. I didn't know whether to go out or not, but Morry came along just then. He took off his coat and put it around her. He's a sweet guy. I don't know what this hotel would do without him. He took her back toward her room. You and Bill ought to do something, Sheep. Your dream child's pretty unhappy. You'd better look into it."

The picture of the tiger-kitten, claws drawn, reduced to lonely tears, submitting docilely to the gnarled kindliness of the old night watchman at four-thirty in the morning, was disturbing in more ways than one. Chiefly it was just the fact of her presence there. There wasn't any doubt that Captain Crawford had left an observer on the spot. He was too shrewd not to have, after his comments on Mrs. Kersey's lighting effects. George Gannon at least had had the good sense to slip around the back way under cover of the shrubbery. Molly should have done the same. And if she'd talked to Mrs. Kersey the way she did to me when she thought I was the lady, Bill and Sheep would probably be visiting her in the County jail before the day was over.

I got up and put on my dressing gown to wait for Sheep to bring my breakfast. The sound of my moving around must have reminded Mrs. Ansell that her closet door was open. I heard her close it, and when the phone rang again it was a distant buzz. I was a little sorry. If she kept the closet door closed I'd never know whether she ever got to talk to Miss Turner or not . . . and I'd be deprived of a seeing eye, and a friendly one, apparently, since she'd reported to Sheep rather than to the police. On the whole it seemed to me that Molly McShane had a fairly wide circle of chaperones. If Mrs. Ansell and Rose, the maid, were aware of Sheep and Bill's interest in her, it was fairly certain all of the more or less permanent guests and employees knew it too. Why she should need any further guardianship it was difficult to see, though it's no doubt a wise provision of California law in general.

I was hoping Sheep and Bill had abandoned their fantastic idea that I would have myself constituted her official overseer when Sheep knocked and came in with my tray. He was so sober-faced that for a moment I wavered. If anything I could do within reason would bring back the infectious grin he'd had when I first saw him, and relieve the load on his mind, which was no doubt equally heavy on Bill's, perhaps I really ought to do it. It seemed a shame to have their "deal," which had been so much fun, go so sour all of a sudden.

"About this guardianship business, Sheep," I began.

He shook his head. "Too late."

"Too late?"

He nodded as he put my tray down on the coffee table and handed me the check.

"Is it Mrs. Kersey?"

"No. Just the general mess. I met Captain Crawford out there when I was coming in. He had the autopsy report. She tripped, all right, and it wasn't on any vine. There's a mark on her instep and they're hunting a piece of hemp cord. The vine was a stall. Mrs. Kersey's trying to tell them she's psychic. That's her story, and Crawford says he doesn't see why she'd want to lie about it. He figures it must have been put there for her, so why should she lie? Anyway, we think it's better to just lie low. So keep quiet about it, will you, Mrs. Latham? And I've got to go. I've got four more break-fasts to get out."

At the door he turned. "Bill won't be here till noon. He's got three classes. Crawford let him off the morning line-up."

"Where's Molly?"

"They're shooting over in the Valley today. She'll be back around one, I guess. Mr. Gannon's producing, but he's not going over. He's still in bed. And he'll be tearing out the telephone wires if I don't get his two-minute eggs and boiled milk in to him. I'll see you later."

I had the feeling that it was less his anxiety to keep Mr. George Gannon from flying into a frenzy than it was his own desire to get away. He'd scarcely closed the door when he opened it again.

"Yeah, she's in here."

I heard an ecstatic "Darling!" and Lucille Gannon burst into the room.

CHAPTER ELEVEN

"GRACE! How wonderful to see you—I didn't even go home to change. Tell me what happened! They're all making like deaf mutes down in the lobby. We just got the tail end of it on the plane when somebody switched the program. I was furious . . . Darling, you look divine! I always look like hell in the morning."

As a matter of fact she did, somewhat. But I doubted if the time of day had much to do with it. She was a lot thinner than she'd been when I saw her in Washington in the spring. Her beige gabardine suit was trim and well cut, but it made her eyes seem paler than their usual almost cat's-eye amber, and the pancake suntan makeup didn't cover the lines around her mouth and chin as well as a few extra over-all pounds of flesh would have done. Her chestnut hair was pulled Chinese tight and she had enough heavy gold chains around her neck and wrist to pass as the mine owner's favorite slave-girl anywhere. But still I thought I was glad to see her. I didn't know what trying to keep up with Hollywood glamor could do to a woman who'd always been glamor personified in the less competitive circles she'd moved in around Washington and Upperville, Va.

"Palm Springs was ghastly, it rained all the time. But do tell me what happened, Grace. Then I'll tell you a secret. Gee Gee's right here in the hotel! He's working like crazy on a new script. But he's dying to meet you. He's completely incommunicado. It's the only way he gets any work done. He always works in a hotel—he says it's the only really impersonal place in the world, the only place where nobody can disturb you. So I just pick up and go some place."

She'd been looking at my breakfast. "I'm going to get some coffee. I had a cup on the plane, but I'm starving." She whipped over to the phone. That done, she flopped down in the big yellow chair across from me. "Now tell me, Grace. What happened? I won't say another word."

"Nobody knows, exactly, Lucille," I said. "A girl was tight, and she fell or tripped—nobody seems absolutely sure—down the stone steps out here. She was killed instantly, they think."

"Oh, dear, isn't that a shame. Who was it? Somebody in the hotel?"

"Not a guest. I don't know whether she even dined here or not."

"Well!" Lucille said, lightly. "All I hope is, it wasn't a string tied across the steps that she tripped over."

I looked at her, startled. "Why?"

"Oh, because then they'd try to pin it on Gee Gee. He's doing a wonderful picture where the heavy murders an old sweetheart of his. It's marvellous. Of course, they use a woman acrobat and the steps are padded and just painted to look like stone. It was an original idea of Gee Gee's, he got it out of a story of Agatha Christie's. He wanted to have a perfectly simple murder that anybody could do, not all complicated and psychological."

"In that case I'd keep it to myself," I said. "The police have an idea that's exactly what happened."

She looked at me blankly. "You mean . . ."

"I mean the police think the girl tripped over a cord that was tied across the stone steps. Only these steps were real stone and the girl wasn't an acrobat. They seem to think it wasn't meant for her but for a woman named Kersey. Viola Van Zant, she used to be. Her room's at the bottom of the steps and she was out at the time."

Lucille sat motionless . . . for the first time, I imagined, in all her life. She needed that heavy suntan pancake makeup.

"You mean Viola Van Zant . . . the . . . the old silent——"

I nodded.

"But Gee Gee . . . he hasn't seen her for years! He's working . . . he wouldn't know whether she was in the hotel or not. He never leaves his room. Anyway, he's always up on the top terrace where it's quiet."

She tried to brush it all aside. "Anyway, that's absurd. Gee Gee——"

She stopped as there was a tap on the door and Sheep came in with her coffee. It was on a large tray that had another breakfast on it. There were two eggs and a dish of something that looked like grated carrots and was grated carrots. There was a thermos jug and a glass but no cup and saucer except the one Sheep took off for Lucille and put with the coffee pot on the table.

Lucille's shoulders stiffened almost as if an electric shock had gone through them. "Is . . . is that boiled milk, Sheep?" She asked the question abruptly and lifted the top of the jug before he had a chance to answer her. "Who's it for?"

"It's for a Mr. Smith."

"What room is Mr. Smith in?"

"101, just across the hall." Sheep glanced at me and gave his head a barely perceptible shake. Lucille didn't even see the check he was holding out to her. I took it and signed it. He'd no sooner closed the door than she was across the room. She put her head against the door, listening, and came back. After a moment she got up again, went to the french window opening on the patio and stood there, like a cat intent on the patter of little mouse feet. And apparently Gee Gee liked his morning carrots in the fresh air. Subdued voices came over the fuchsia-showered white brick wall. When she came back and sat down she was subdued too, so subdued that she'd forgotten about her coffee. I poured a cup for her.

"You'd better drink this."

"Listen to me," she said abruptly. "Don't get any silly notions in your head. Gee Gee wouldn't try to kill Viola Van Zant. I wouldn't tell anybody else this, but the truth is he's never got over being in love with her. It's the absolute truth. You know she was his second wife."

I hadn't known it. I don't seem to manage to keep *au courant* in this shifting world.

"They were divorced, but that was because he wasn't making any money, and she was washed up in pictures. He thought it was only fair to let her marry someone with a lot of money while she had the chance."

"Modern chivalry," I remarked. I didn't entirely mean to, but it seemed a quaint conception of marital responsibility.

"Oh, out here money's awfully important. It really is, Grace. I know a writer who says people ought to have their salary printed on a tag to wear in their lapel so you don't make a mistake and speak to the wrong person. Anyway, Gee Gee's never been as much in love with anybody else. It's just one of those things that happen to people. So you see he wouldn't do her any harm. You see that, don't you, Grace? It would be horrible. No matter how much she'd hurt him, he'd never want to hurt her. And even if we knew she was going to be in Hollywood, he wouldn't know she was in this hotel."

"Did you know?" I asked.

She nodded. "We'd heard she was coming. I knew before Gee Gee did. Eustace told me. He said she had a lot of dough she wanted to throw away, and I couldn't have been more pleased."

She picked up her coffee cup.

"Anyway, Grace, Viola Van Zant isn't dead, is she? So if she isn't dead, Gee Gee can't be accused of killing her, very well, can he?"

It seemed to settle everything beautifully, in Lucille's mind. She relaxed back into her chair.

"I think you're right about that," I said. "There is the small matter of the girl who was killed."

"But darling, don't be absurd! That doesn't concern Gee Gee. That's ridiculous. Quite frankly, Grace, I don't see what on earth we're getting all so upset about, either one of us. I should think the best thing to do is say nothing about it. And I think I'd better go home."

She picked up her bag, went over to the door and stopped to draw on her gloves. "Have you met Molly McShane yet?" she inquired casually, without looking at me.

"Yes," I said. "I've met her several times."

"She's one of Gee Gee's finds."

She was still being elaborately casual about it.

"I believe you called her a trollop, in your letter to me about Bill," I said. "All kinds of a trollop, as I remember."

"Oh well. You know me." She shrugged lightly, smoothing the back of her glove with more interest than it deserved. "I get burned up about things and get over it the next day. Bill and Sheep had the cockeyed idea I'd like to act as some kind of legal guardian for my husband's coming star. They must take me for a damned fool. I'd wreck my marriage for a bright idea of theirs! Not much I wouldn't. If it *was* their idea—which I doubt. I suspect it was that rat Eustace Sype's, the whole thing from beginning to end—including the juke box joint where they're supposed to have picked her up. It's a good publicity gag, or they're two of the world's outstanding suckers."

"Why do you say that?"

"Do you know anything about Molly McShane?" she demanded. She'd dropped any pretense of being casual and disinterested.

I shook my head. "Only what the boys have told me."

"Then you'd better get busy, that's all I can tell you. I don't want to suggest that anybody's paying your son to be a gigolo, but it wouldn't be the first time it's happened. You know Eustace Sype as well as I do. And of course it's none of my business, but if Bill was my son, I'd darn well want to know a lot more about the girl he and Sheep take turns dragging to all the hot spots than anybody here pretends he knows."

"I take it you don't like Molly McShane, Lucille," I said.

"You take it quite right, darling. I don't like her. I don't like anything about her. I don't like the way she lands on my doorstep and takes Gee Gee in, so he goes all out and almost loses his top star because he pushes Molly right into the camera as if *she* was his leading lady. No, I don't like her. And you watch. The first chance she gets, she'll ditch Bill and Sheep, and if it *is* their own money they're spending on her . . ."

She shrugged again. "They'll have their memories. That girl is the spit of her mother."

"Do you know her mother?"

"No. How would I know her mother? I don't move in those circles."

Then, as if realizing it was unbecoming to engender quite so much heat over somebody who shouldn't matter quite that much, she did a nice job of thermic control.

"But I know something about her. Eustace Sype told me. For instance—I know she stole a diamond bracelet that belonged to Viola Van Zant. Or half of it did. The other half belonged to Gee Gee, under community property rights. And you needn't tell Bill and Sheep I told you . . . nor Gee Gee."

I looked at her. "You mean he doesn't know? You haven't told him? If it's true, or important, I should think——"

She stopped me with a brief ironic glance. "I'm not a fool, darling. Men don't believe things about the other woman—not when their wife tells them. If I told Gee Gee, he'd probably go out and buy her a diamond bracelet himself, to atone for her parents' sin, and insist I take over her guardianship. It's a chance I'm not taking, angel— because knowing Eustace I haven't the slightest doubt exactly what he had in mind. He thought I'd run straight to Gee Gee."

And again as if she thought I might take a dim view of her intensity about it, she laughed lightly.

"I expect Eustace thought I couldn't take anybody's getting away with my half of a diamond bracelet. But I'm smarter than he thinks.

Anyway, you just ask him. There's no dirt that's been spilled here for twenty years that Eustace doesn't know all about. He's a magnet that attracts it and a squirrel that stores it. And if he doesn't want to talk, you just bring out your club and let him have it."

"My club?" I asked.

"His book, darling. Remember *The Coming of Age of E. P. S.?* It's the one thing he's really ashamed of. He's psychotic about it. Nobody here knows he ever wrote a book—and they'd laugh their heads off. It would absolutely ruin Stinky, and he knows it. I've got six copies of it, in a safe. It's the only way I get along with him. He's scared to death of me. So go see him, dear. He'll talk."

"He doesn't get up till four o'clock," I said.

"Rot. He gets up in plenty of time to gouge the studios with the moth-eaten talent he handles. But don't get me started on Stinky Sype. He certainly got himself a fine package deal when he got the little McShane. Sheep and Bill to tote her around, Gee Gee to give her a part and put her across, and . . . well, I'd better shut up. You just go and see him, Grace. Unless you're a lot dumber than I think you are you ought to be able to put a few things together."

She put her hand on the doorknob.

"I hate this place, Grace. I wish to God I'd never come here."

I started to tell her to be careful going out. The girl from Seattle had said much the same thing, though without such intense bitterness. And she wasn't angry, and Lucille was.

"As a matter of fact, I love it," she said more quietly. "That's the hell of it. Everybody that says he hates it is really crazy about it. It gets in your blood and you can't stay away from it. It's when you're not a success in it that you pretend you hate it."

"Aren't you a success, dear?"

I meant it to sound lighter than it did, or than she took it, anyway. The sharp lines around her mouth looked suddenly as if they'd been cut with a knife in fresh suntan plaster.

"Nobody's ever decided what success is, out here," she said, after a moment's silence. "If you're a woman, it's age twenty-two. If you could figure something to keep you always twenty-two . . . that would be success. And no woman's ever achieved it. But I'm going. If you should see Gee Gee—no, don't bother. I'll tell his secretary to tell him I'm home. I wish I'd stayed in Palm Springs."

She opened the door, and pushed it quickly shut.

"The police are out there, Grace . . . and Gee Gee's door is open. Oh, this is horrible! The reporters . . . the papers will . . ."

She looked desperately around, and pointed to the french window. "Does that . . . where does that go to? Can I——?"

"You can try it," I said. I didn't tell her her husband had found it a way out in the early hours of the morning, and that the dead girl had found it a way in before that.

She dropped a kiss on the top of my head as she hurried past me. "—I know I sound horrible, Grace . . . but wait till you've been here as long as I have."

I did wait about ten minutes, half expecting her to reappear, but as she didn't I took a shower and got dressed. So far there had been no summons from Captain Crawford, and I saw no reason for barging out until I had to. And I was concerned about Lucille. On her flying sorties into Washington, she was a blithe spirit, her life in Hollywood rainbow-hued and full of such excitement and glamor that it made life on the Potomac seem like a crust of moldy bread.

It's proverbial, of course, that an angry woman is not a reliable reporter either of event or of character. Still, Lucille's attitude toward her Gee Gee and Viola Kersey appeared so rational and adult, compared to the intensity of her bitterness toward little Molly McShane, that I decided I'd take her advice and see what was behind it all. If Eustace Sype or anybody else was playing Bill and Sheep for a couple of suckers, as she'd put it, the quicker I knew it the better. Not that I'd be able to stop it, I supposed, or convince them of it, but I'd at least have the satisfaction of knowing what the score was.

And I got it at Eustace Sype's house in Bel Air that afternoon. There was no satisfaction in it, and it wasn't the whole score. The blood-drenched figures were not all in, at that point. But I did get two exceedingly important digits of the score. I also got why Sheep Clarke said it was too late to do anything about guardianship for Molly McShane. He and Bill were very wise when they decided it was better to just lie low. The question was how low could they lie . . . how long could they lie there.

CHAPTER TWELVE

At eleven o'clock Captain Crawford sent for me. Viola Kersey, George Gannon and I were the only ones present in the assistant manager's office. What seemed to me a quaint local custom was in effect. Nat, the bellboy, wasn't there because it was his day off and he was spending it in jail as his third weekly contribution to a ten-day sentence he was working out for reckless driving. Molly McShane wasn't there because she was working, and Bill because he had classes. I'd never heard of the police fitting themselves to anybody else's occupational convenience before, but it seemed like a sound idea. Rose and Morry Shavin weren't there because they worked nights and slept in the morning. It didn't seem to matter a great deal, however. They had not yet found out who the dead girl was. Until she was reported missing or someone recognized her picture in the papers and came forward, all they knew was that she was about twenty-five years old, had a job of some kind, came from Seattle, Washington, and had met her death while under the influence of alcohol by tripping over a piece of hemp cord on the stone steps of the Casa del Flores. If Captain Crawford knew any more, he was keeping it to himself.

Viola Kersey was sticking calmly to her story about the vine. It must have taken a good deal of will power to resist the natural temptation to improve it, now she'd had a long time to think it over. Or perhaps it was her training in reading lines the way they were written. If the night watches had not changed the lines of her story, however, they had very much changed the lines of her face. Its pliant cooing softness had settled into a solid and watchful determination. Whatever it was Mrs. Kersey wanted, it was clear she had got it, and all she had to do was keep it. Her self-confidence was superb. She would never have appeared in a pair of powder-blue gabardine slacks if it hadn't been. Her mink coat and sun glasses were merely finishing touches, as was the glittering load of sapphires she bore, distributed at various strategic positions on her person.

Beside her milk and corn-fed opulence, Gee Gee Gannon looked like a man raddled with ulcers and despair.

"You now say you did talk to her," Captain Crawford remarked. "Last night——"

"I know what I said last night," George Gannon retorted irritably. "I said I hadn't seen her and hadn't talked to her. And you'd do the same in my place. I never see the girl before she turns up on my patio. She says she's hunting somebody who has her bag. I see she's tight. That doesn't make any difference to me. It can be a stall, just like the bag. In this business women are so much poison ivy. There's nothing they won't do, and we get the fireworks. I have trouble enough without getting saddled with any I'm not looking for."

"Anyway, I'd just come, hadn't I, George?" Viola Kersey said sweetly. The implication was sour enough. It also explained why she'd had to rap on his door more than once to be let in. "You see, Captain, Mr. Gannon and I are old friends. We were married for several years, at one time. Three, wasn't it, George? I've forgotten. And I was *so* surprised, and *so* pleased, when I found out he was here . . . alone."

I couldn't tell about the surprise part of it, but if George G. Gannon shared the pleasure angle he concealed it to a noteworthy degree. The impression I got was that he'd like to boil Mrs. Viola Kersey in rancid oil, thereafter dumping her into the nethermost of the nethermost reaches, to continue burning through all eternity and beyond. That was the way he looked, certainly. I'd thought he was heavy-set, seeing him briefly when he was out in the hall demanding where the hell his ice was, the evening before. Now I saw it was just the paunchiness of the sedentary worker. Though Mr. Gannon could not properly be called sedentary. He was in and out of his chair now, across the narrow room and back, up and down and around twenty times in five minutes. He was shaved, and he had a bright checked coat on over his black open-collared sport shirt. Whether it was the same cigar or a new one I didn't know, but he had a fascinating technique of gnashing it from one corner of his mouth to the other, as if his teeth were equipped with trolley tracks, and suddenly grabbing it out and gesticulating with it before he jammed it back. He was like an animated cartoon in a bad temper with St. Vitus dance. How he stood the strain he put on himself seemed miraculous to me unless grated carrots are good for more than night blindness and curly hair. His hair, however, was mostly gone, I had no doubt because he'd torn it out by the roots with his own bare hands.

And yet I had the impression that somewhere back of all this frenetic hopping and seething was a genuinely nice guy, but one so harassed by intrigue, real or imagined, and the frantic pace he lived at, that he simply didn't dare relax. The way his bright peeled brown eyes popped out at me as he snapped his head forward to acknowledge Captain Crawford's introduction led me to believe his wife was exaggerating when she said he was dying to meet me. I didn't mind, however, because it was all too obvious that my presence wasn't the supreme irritant. It was Viola Kersey's, which was no doubt the reason I was sure there was a heart of quiet gold concealed somewhere behind all the irascible jumps and jerks. His eyes were popping at Mrs. Kersey now as Captain Crawford asked if she'd expected to see him in the hotel.

"Never!" cried Mrs. Kersey. "Never in the whole wide world. I did call his office, but his secretary said he was in Palm Springs with his wife. It was entirely by accident I learned he was here. The telephone operator was sending a telegram over the switchboard. I always think other people's telegrams are so interesting, so I listened. One was to Mrs. George G. Gannon in Palm Springs. She spelled out the signature, 'Gee Gee,' and said the room charge was 101."

She smiled at Captain Crawford, ingenuously. "So it was quite a coincidence, although I so often think coincidence is only the unbeliever's way of admitting the hand of fate in our puny lives."

I had the feeling that it was almost more than George Gannon could take. And Mrs. Kersey then turned her coconut-cream smile on him. "I do think 'Gee Gee' is awfully sweet, and so perfect for you, George dear. Perhaps if I'd thought of that our marriage would never have ended the way it did."

I thought it would probably have ended with a shotgun or old-fashioned razor and George happily doing the last mile up to the Thirteen Steps, if his present state was any indication of an earlier one. If I were Viola Kersey, I thought, I'd shut my mouth and take the next train back to Chicago. But she was enormously pleased with herself. She had her former husband right on the griddle where it was hottest, and exactly where she wanted him.

"You see," she said, "it was not a *personal* call, Captain. It was entirely business. My husband, Samuel C. Kersey, of the Kersey

Foods Incorporated, has given me a few pennies to play with. I'm so interested in the motion picture indus· y, and an independent producer like Mr. Gannon is exactly w.... i'm hunting for. I have a story, too, and the girl I want to play it is under contract to George. So I think we're going to be able to do something. George is really most enthusiastic about it. And I'm a very *good* business woman, Captain. Have you seen this girl Molly McShane they were talking about last night?"

She didn't look at me, nor did George Gannon. Captain Crawford did, briefly, before he turned without answering the question to George.

"You admit now you did see this girl."

"That's right, I do admit it, but I don't want the papers screaming it all over the country. I don't want my wife to get the idea I hole in here for any flapdoodle. I come here to work, by God, and I don't want everybody from Maine to Florida thinking I'm not working. These damned reporters and columnists'll crucify you."

Mr. Gannon jumped up and spread his arms out to show us. Then he jumped around the other way, jabbing his cigar at Captain Crawford.

"Here I'm working. This girl barges in. This girl I never see before. So she's tight. So she's lost her bag. So what? I gotta get her out before somebody else comes in. I gotta get her out before everybody from Maine to Florida yells, hey, what's he doing with a dame in his room when he says he's working? What's he doing? So I'm getting her out when Viola comes. I'm getting her out and keeping my mouth shut. I'm not telling anybody! Police . . . anybody! See?"

His idea that a minor incident in his private existence would have such impact as to rock the East Coast seemed to me distorted, but I live a secluded life. That his ulcers were due for a more soothing diet than his raw produce was something to be considered, however. He was all over the room acting his parts—the girl, Viola, and the population of the Eastern seaboard—before he dropped into his chair.

Mrs. Kersey smiled at him again. "I wouldn't have told a soul, Georgie dear. I have a clean mind. I assumed it was your wife, darling."

I thought he was going into another state, but he just looked as if he could have strangled her with the utmost pleasure.

"Well, there's no use you two quarrelling," Captain Crawford said amicably. "Especially if you're going into business together. I expect that's what you were down talking about, around three o'clock, was it, Mr. Gannon? One of my boys says he saw you."

George Gannon clenched his fists and drew in his breath and held it. He exhaled it with terrific self-control.

"Look. Look, Captain Crawford. I'm trying to go to sleep. You come in. You tell me this girl's dead on the steps. You're going. I'm trying to go to sleep another time. I'm nearly crazy, not knowing what this dame's got in her mind. I get up. I take a shower. I take a drink. I take another drink. I'm nearly crazy. I decide I'll go see her. I want to see what she's after. If I go the front way I run into your flatfeet. So I go the back way. I go in her house. She's got on every light in the place. She's in the bathroom with the door locked. So she comes out. And to make a long story short, she says she's going to break my contract with Molly McShane. She says you play ball or I take Molly. This I don't like. This makes me see red. And then she says we do business together!"

George Gannon flung his arms up with special violence.

"What about those lights, Mrs. Kersey? It isn't that you're worried about anything, is it?"

"No. I like lights."

"So you have a chair and pillow in the bathroom?" George Gannon demanded. "And the door locked—because you like light."

I thought that for an instant Viola Kersey felt little more kindly toward him than he did toward her. But she covered up quickly.

"Well, Gee Gee. You were so cross at me, dear, and you've got such a violent temper. I thought I'd feel a little safer . . ."

"So you opened the bathroom door and came out and talked to him."

"Yes, of course, Captain. I knew your men were outside. He wouldn't dare do anything, with them around."

She smiled sweetly at him. Captain Crawford hesitated a moment. "All right. I'll see you all later." He turned to me. "Just check this statement you made last night, Mrs. Latham. See if there's anything you want to change or amplify."

It was the police stenographer's report, all neatly typed, and there was nothing I wanted to add or change. All I wanted to do was get out and go over to Eustace Sype's. It seemed even more important now than it had before, and I was naive enough to assume that all I had to do was look in the telephone book. He wasn't listed, of course, nor were the George G. Gannons. But that was reasonable, as it was obvious Gee Gee wouldn't want everybody from Maine to Florida able to call him up as the impulse seized them. I might have asked him, but I didn't have a chance. He strode past me along the flagstone path without speaking, disguised in dark glasses, which was also reasonable considering the trouble he had escaping the Pursuit of Women.

It was one-thirty before the simple expedient of asking the girl at the desk occurred to me. She put in a call for a taxi, which was how I saw Molly McShane in a totally new light.

She was sitting on the low white brick wall under the entrance awning. I didn't recognize her at first. She looked like any bobby-soxer from Los Angeles to Baltimore waiting for the school bus. Her hair was slicked back and caught with a curved barette at the nape of her neck. She had on a blue sweater and plaid shirt, scuffed brown moccasins and short white socks. A camel's hair coat was on the wall beside her, one book on top of it and another open on her crossed knee. She was chewing her pencil and looking as dejected as all her class when confronted with the grim problem of unfinished home work. The bright red polish was gone from her finger nails and her lipstick was of a much milder hue than it had been the day before. She glanced up as I came down the walk, a pretty unhappy and disturbed kid, nothing defiant or sultry about her.

"Hello, Molly," I said.

"Hello, Mrs. Latham. Have you seen Sheep? He's supposed to take me to school."

I looked at her books. One was the *Elements of Euclid*, the other *Plato's Dialogues*. I must have looked as startled as I was.

"That's Sheep and Bill," she said. "They say I have to train my mind."

She said it so dolefully and without inner conviction that I didn't know whether to laugh or cry.

"You only *have* to finish high school out here, but Sheep and Bill say I have to do two years at U. C. L. A. They say it makes a lot of difference, some way."

The idea of my son and his shipmate having developed such academic standards was something. The contrast between that and

Lucille Gannon's harrowing alarums and excursions over their moral disintegration seemed to me fairly typical of the trend of middle age deploring the youth. If Molly was a trollop, I thought, she had certainly fallen into the hands of a couple of Platonic wolves. I felt really sorry for the poor lamb. She put *Euclid* on top of the *Dialogues* and sat studying her folded hands.

"I'm sorry about last night, Mrs. Latham," she said slowly. "I had a letter in my bag I didn't want anybody to see. It would have made a terrible lot of trouble for . . . for everybody. For just *everybody*. I didn't want Sheep and Bill to be worried about it. They've been so sweet to me I didn't want them to think . . . well, they might have thought somebody was double-crossing them. And it isn't true. It *really* isn't. But it's bound to look like it. I guess that's the reason it's always best to tell the truth in the first place, isn't it? That's what Socrates would have said. I guess that's one of the reasons it's good to train your mind. You find out that people knew the same answers a long time ago, don't you?"

She looked up at me, her eyes a little blind and tearful. She swallowed and looked down at her quiescent hands again.

"It's just all so miserable," she said simply. "It makes it look like we were lying to them. I said we . . . we ought to tell them. Because it's not our fault really. We did the best we could. It was the only way we knew."

"What do you mean, Molly?"

"Well, I mean . . ."

She looked up quickly. A cab was streaking into the driveway. It skidded around on the outside of two wheels and came to a stop in front of us.

"You ladies 102, Room 102? Mrs. Latham?"

The moment when I might have got the truth from a subdued and contrite Molly McShane was gone. The driver had whipped out and opened the door for me. Molly was blowing her nose and sniffling a little.

"Where to, lady?"

"Saks-Fifth Avenue," I said. It was the only place I could think of quickly, knowing nothing about Los Angeles. If I'd given him the address I had in Bel Air, I doubt if Molly could have sat there so meekly. When we came to the parked intersection at the end of the Canyon I gave him Eustace Sype's address.

Before we got to Stone Canyon Road a low-slung dilapitated monster streaked by us. It had a sheep's head and a billy goat's head painted on the back. The Sheep was at the wheel, Molly beside him. I took it my son, the goat, was doing his staggered shift with trays and things back at the hotel.

"That's one of them hot rods," the driver said. "They ought to be a law. But I guess they don't kill themselves unless they get in too big a hurry."

"Where's U. C. L. A.?" I asked.

He waved his arm out to the left to an enormous straggling plain of pseudo-Byzantine buildings lying below us as we turned right into Stone Canyon Road. And from then until we ended way up on top of the immediate world I heard what the Trojans were going to do to the Illini—were going to do, but didn't. I've always been a little sorry about the driver's hundred bucks. At the moment I was concerned about how Sheep, after delivering Molly for her mental training, was going to get to Pasadena without getting in too big a hurry . . . and about how I was going to get inside the raspberry stuccoed mansion with the forbidding raspberry stuccoed wall flanked with mountains of a blue flowering stuff that has a name that sounds like lumbago and that I've never seen anywhere else.

I had a copy of *The Coming of Age of E. P. S.*, but it was in the attic of the yellow brick house on P Street in Georgetown, and I was at E. P. S.'s front gate in Bel Air. I got out. The gate was open a foot or so, with a large sign that said *Private, No Tourists*. I went in and up the white coral roadway to the front door—*Private. Beware of the Dogs*. I could hear them yapping like mad inside the house as I rang the door bell and set up a series of tintinabulations that sounded like all the temple bells of the forbidden city. And to my great surprise, Eustace Sype opened the door.

I could tell it was Eustace by the sheer breadth and poundage, because otherwise he looked very odd. He had on a white embroidered mandarin robe, red slippers with their toes turned up, and a curious little hat that I presumed was also Chinese. Pekinese dogs swarmed around him like a cloud of pug-nosed bumble bees.

"Darling, how sweet of you to come! Dear Lucille phoned me to expect you. Hasn't she turned into a dreary type? I'm so fond of her. Do come in, dear. You'll forgive my servantless house—they were called away on business. This way, darling."

He waddled in front of me to a pair of black-lacquered doors and pushed them open into an enormous room that opened out into the most extraordinary panorama of ocean, city and mountains, or would have if a heavy smog, as they call it, hadn't obscured everything below us. The room itself was what I imagine a sybaritic sultan of the Chinese Ottoman Empire would admire, and lovely in a way, although my knees creak when I sit on overstuffed divans six inches from the floor. Eustace fluttered a white hand for me to sit on an old gold brocaded one some ten feet from the cherry-red silk one that was apparently reserved for him. It had a back and one side, the other side missing so he could reach out to a low teakwood table on which there were carved jade and silver ornaments and a jade box of perfumed cigarettes. The cherry-red throne seat, as it were, was like a billowing feather bed fluffed out, not a crease or wrinkle in it.

It was basically also about six inches from the floor, and how Eustace was going to get into it without the aid of an electric crane I didn't see. I was fascinated at the way he did it. He reminded me of Queen Victoria who never had to look to see if her chair was there . . . it always had been, it always would be. Eustace's own derrière was royal to that extent. He stood fluttering me to my place, and then he gave his silken shod hoofs an absurd little outward thrust on the polished floor and sank, collapsing into his down cushions, lolling there luxuriously, his dogs around him, a grotesque occidental buddha, white against the cherry-red damask squeezing itself out around him.

He surveyed me then, a humorous and not wholly unmalicious smile under his curved-up eyebrows.

"What can I do for you, Grace darling?"

CHAPTER THIRTEEN

PUT SO SIMPLY, it was hard for me to say what it was I wanted and have any hope of an honest answer, now that Lucille had taken all the surprise element out of my visit.

"You can tell me about Viola Kersey," I said.

"Viola Kersey? Oh, dear."

At least I'd surprised him with that question.

"Dear Vi. She's such a bore, isn't she. A really profound bore. But she has a great deal of money. Which gives her a certain patina. Go away, boys and girls. Go away. Go away quickly!"

He took his hands out of his sleeves and fluttered them around, shooing the flock of Pekinese off his person and place. They flew pell mell out of the open windows onto the terrace.

"Quiet, boys and girls," he called. As they shut their yapping off like so many little spigots, he turned to me again.

"Viola has a great deal of money. I hope we can relieve her of a large chunk of it. That's what I was discussing with her last evening. She wants to settle herself in Hollywood. Frankly, I think she's yearning to get back at a few people she feels didn't appreciate her. And then, of course . . ."

Eustace shrugged.

"Her husband is making fabulous amounts purveying congealed foods to hoi polloi, and dear Viola feels she might as well have the fun of throwing it away herself instead of having the government do it for her. It's quite simple, darling. It's done with race horses and scientific yachting expeditions, *and* with motion pictures. I think dear Viola's really going to enjoy herself."

He looked at me thoughtfully.

"And make restitution, in a sense."

"Restitution?"

"Precisely, darling. I think the dear girl feels she treated poor old Gannon pretty shabbily, so she's chosen him for her producer. He needs the money. Dear, dear . . . we all need the money. She has it."

Eustace shrugged again and smiled at me, squinting up his globular face in a very un-Chinese fashion, except that his eyes were still as warm as bits of green jade.

"Yes, I think it's a highly satisfactory arrangement for all of us. Especially for Molly. She's such a sweet child, isn't she?"

The face was wreathed in that specious smile again, but the eyes were bright and intently fixed on me, calculating, weighing my reactions with completely scientific detachment.

"How does it affect Molly?" I asked.

"Oh, dear. I do wish people's emotions didn't so befog their business acumen," Eustace Sype said plaintively. "I don't mean you, dear. I'm so glad you're here, because you can be a very real help to us all. You see Viola can do so much for dear little Molly. Let's be completely realistic about it. It's for her own good. I'm sure if someone like yourself could explain it to those two charming young men they would see it in its true light. I'm sure they would never for an instant stand in her way. They must realize that delightful though their adventure has been, it can't go on. I'm really afraid, Grace, they're neglecting their studies, and working nights I'm afraid for their health. Truly, my dear."

"Nonsense, Stinky," I said, smiling at him. "Cut it in smaller pieces if you really want me to swallow it."

He smiled back. "I thought I could appeal to you as an American Mother, Grace dear. And I much prefer you don't call me Stinky. I spend a large sum yearly on the better-class deodorants. But practically, dear: Viola plans to buy a little place here in Bel Air. I know one that's available for a mere two hundred thousand that would be a lovely setting for our young lady. She could have furs and jewels and clothes and a suitable car without the usual bother, and——"

"What's in it for Viola Kersey? What does she get out of it? What's she doing it for?"

"Spite, dear. Just sheer unmitigated spite."

Eustace smiled at me again, the false smile, and fluttered his hands.

"—Or perhaps that's unfair. What she gets out of it is glamor. Let's put it that way. She becomes duenna for one of our most promising starlets. She doesn't have to live alone and lure people to her gilded web by mere food and liquor. It's superb publicity for her, now that Hollywood is so domestic and respectable. My dear Grace, it's a natural——"

"Was it you that suggested it, by any chance?"

"Oh dear, dear! I'm so grossly misunderstood always. I would be really distressed if Sheep and Bill got the impression I thought their tutelage was inadequate. You're a practical woman, Grace. You can face facts. You don't truly want your son to fall in love with a girl like Molly, do you? I mean, what of her antecedents? Do you know anything about them?"

"I thought possibly you'd tell me something about them, dear," I said.

"When neither your son nor his friend, Sheep, has done so? Ah! No, my dear. That would be disloyal. Disloyal in the extreme."

"I didn't dream you'd regard that as a plausible excuse, Eustace," I said.

"And you're so right, dear." He spoke with the highest good humor. "I shouldn't, not for an instant, unless there were also genuine reasons. I wouldn't myself dream, however, of being disloyal to a friend if it cost me money, as this would. We're old enough, and have known each other long enough, to be perfectly frank, Grace. And I'm sure you'd never be so stupid as to try to come between your son and people he feels to be his friends."

I was a little annoyed. "I might, as a matter of fact, just give him a copy of your famous book . . ."

Eustace Sype's small jade-hard eyes glanced brittle sparks at me. His rounded jowls had a mottled unhealthy paleness.

"I don't like that, Grace," he said venomously. "I don't like that at all. You and Lucille——"

That was as far as he got. The dogs had been yapping in a sort of off-stage chorus of alarm that Eustace had noticed but ignored when it became joyful greeting. But now the torrential patter of their little feet on the bare floors coming from behind the lacquered doors, and running footsteps with them, couldn't be ignored. Nor could Eustace get himself up from his cherry silk divan to intercept them before the doors burst open.

"–Eustace! Where's my mother? Where's Mother, and where's Dad——?"

It was Molly McShane. She saw me sitting there. For a stupefied instant she was petrified into immobility, her hands still out, holding the black glistening doors apart, the dogs in a noisy sea of ecstatic writhing fur around her feet.

"Boys and girls!" Eustace clapped his hands together. "Quiet!"

They subsided magically. And as magically, Molly came to vibrant passionate life.

"Where are they, Eustace! I don't care if she does know! I don't care who knows! I'm not ashamed of them, and I won't stand this any longer! You can't do this, do you hear me?"

"Oh, come, come, Molly." Eustace rolled his body more comfortably into his cushions. "That's not fit for a fourth-rate *East Lynne*.

Come, come. Stop being absurd. It's a frightful bore. I can't bear corn, darling."

"I don't care if it is a bore."

Her stormy eyes blazed back at him.

"I don't care if it is corny. I mean it. You can't do it, and you're not going to!"

"I'm not going to do what, sweet child?" He spoke with mountainous imperturbability. "I'm afraid I'm old and very dull, today . . . and completely bewildered, my child. What gross evil am I accused of now?"

"Oh, you beast! You beast! You know! You know what I mean, and I hate you! It's your fault—you know it is!"

She broke down in a passion of sobbing, tormented beyond any control. Eustace looked at her with distaste and profound ennui. Then he rolled over a little and tapped on a silver-gilt gong, pagoda-shaped and electrified, I gathered, because it sounded beautifully through the house.

"I personally would never think of trusting Mrs. Latham, Molly, but if you wish to it's your own affair. And I despise melodrama. Nor do I care to be misjudged, my dear child. I assume you're talking about Mrs. Kersey's very kind and generous offer? Is that what all this . . . this sound and fury signify? Correct me if I'm mistaken."

"Kind! Generous!"

Through her storm-torn efforts to control herself, Molly still put all the contempt in the world in those two words.

"And I've asked you to dress yourself properly when you come to this house," Eustace said, tapping the gong again.

He let a distasteful glance move from her scuffed moccasins up to her plaid skirt and blue sweater, and rest on her hair.

"And go to a hairdresser, occasionally."

He tapped the gong again, with irritation this time.

"I was trying to hide your unhappy parents. I went to the trouble of opening the front door with my own hands to save you humiliation." He ignored the savage tension that quivered through her, and motioned her to silence. "But disloyalty is something I've never been accused of, and we'll just settle this right now, Molly my dear. I assure you, dear child, it is not I who am insisting you go with Mrs. Kersey. It isn't at all. It's your own parents."

He snapped the word out and at the same time gave the gong a really healthy bang. I could hear slow footsteps coming toward us. The dogs went into a flurry of delight, cut short by the commanding clap of their master's white hands.

"It is your parents who want you to go with Mrs. Kersey, my child."

He raised his voice, turning his head, waiting for them to appear.

"Oh, Mother!"

The girl ran forward and threw herself into the arms of the dour woman with the lined face. It was the night maid, Rose, from the Casa del Flores, and standing wretchedly there beside her, in a servant's white coat, was Morris Shavin, the Casa del Flores night watchman. Rose held the child to her, looking silently at Eustace.

"Molly thinks it is I who insist she go to Mrs. Kersey, Rose," he said.

"Mother . . . oh, please not, Mother!"

It was all going on around me as if I were pinioned in the grip of a relentless dream, unable to wake. I remembered Rose interrupting the girl at my door the night before, sending her up to her room to sleep, Molly's suddenly deflated acquiescence and obedience that I'd taken as an anti-climax of an interrupted scene . . . and Morry Shavin, the night watchman, putting his coat around the weeping child, leading her docilely to her room from her four-thirty tryst with Viola Kersey.

"You see, Grace, the boys took 'M. Shavin' and made 'McShane' out of it," Eustace said indifferently. "It's more euphonious, don't you think?"

What I did think was that I hated him, at that moment, with almost as much of a sense of frustration and violence as Molly herself did.

"You may go now, Morris. Get us some tea. Use the package that came yesterday. Rose will remain and explain to Molly. I'm sure Rose will make it all quite clear."

Molly drew away from her mother, white-faced and incredulous.

"I don't . . . I don't have to go to her? Please, Mother . . . say I don't! I *hate* her."

There were no dramatics then. She was a child, explaining, and truly confident of understanding and protection. The face of the maid went through a spasm of uncertainty, and hardened into grim determination. I remembered the towels and the pitcher of ice cubes, the abrupt fashion in which Viola Kersey had said "Maid," when she ordered her to bring them to her room, the sullen angry figure that came along the flagstone path bringing them . . . and Viola Kersey's confidence the next morning. I knew what Rose was going to say before she said it.

"You have to go, Molly."

She pushed the two brown hands that flew out to her in appeal roughly away.

"You must go. I've said it, and you must obey."

She moved back, her mouth drawn tightly down. Dour was no longer the word. She was stone, and bitter stone. If her hands hadn't been trembling so she had to clasp them together I would have thought she was a ruthless and awful woman. But I didn't think it. All I thought was, what a horrible price to pay for a stolen bracelet, even if it had had all the diamonds in the world in it.

And then I thought of something else, and for a moment everything seemed strangely quiet. A diamond bracelet, a piece of hemp string . . . Viola Kersey had lost the bracelet. Viola Kersey had found the string.

"Mother!" Molly's voice sounded lost and far away. "I can't, Mother."

"You must go to her, Molly."

The girl's frail little shoulders slumped forward. She bent her head down. Just the line of her body was an abstraction of a concept of obedience and submission that Heaven knows few parents of today could demand and get, and that few would require. It was a strangely moving and pathetic moment. Eustace, who I'm sure felt nothing of it, shattered it with a sudden double clap of his hands.

"All right, boys and girls!" The dogs, who'd been sitting like so many little frozen puppets, burst into an hysterical frolic. "Go with Rose!" They jumped and scrambled at her skirt. "We'd like some rice cakes, Rose, and tell Morris not to bother with tea. We'll have some of the rice wine, I think. Will you sit down and join us, Molly dear? If not, you can run along home. Rose has a good deal of work to do. She has to see the police at some fantastic hour this afternoon. But do stay, dear."

"No, thank you."

Molly spoke very quietly, and as quickly crossed the room and went out the black lacquered doors.

CHAPTER FOURTEEN

EUSTACE pulled a painted ivory fan from one of his embroidered sleeves and moved it indolently in front of his face once or twice.

"You see what I mean, dear Grace. Emotions are a luxury that the poor can't afford to have. Rose is a sensible and ambitious woman. She wants the best for her daughter. I think it's all very commendable, don't you, dear?"

"I think it would be better if I didn't say what I think, Eustace."

I had to get up. I knew my knee joints were going to creak and make my exit seem a little absurd. But I had to chance it, and my pent-up fury must have secreted some annealing fluid, because I managed without indignity.

"And I think I'll go now. Goodbye."

"If you'll wait I'll call a taxi. I shall need my own car."

"I'd rather walk, I think."

Eustace Sype got very slowly to his feet. How he did it I didn't see and, as it was the one opportunity I was likely to have, it was a distinct loss, if I'd ever had any interest in the operation of large but movable bodies. I was only interested in getting out of that malevolent house.

"Of course you understand, Grace," Eustace said. "I'm sure you understand, dear. If I were in the least alarmed at your possible interest, we would have played the scene somewhere else. I allowed you to see it merely to impress you with the fact that your interference would be both untimely and dangerous. I have no doubt Lucille told you that Rose was dear Viola's maid, and Morris her chef, when Viola was married to poor old Georgie Gannon. Viola has a genuinely sweet and forgiving spirit. She wouldn't think of making trouble for either of the dear souls."

His hands fluttered.

"I was so happy when I discovered that their child would be able to make the recompense for them. Viola has been *most* patient."

He waddled after me to the front steps.

"I dare say there are some people who would regard it as most unfortunate that dear Viola didn't go down the stone steps before that wretched young woman got so foolishly muddled about the way out of the hotel, last night. I hope no one suggests to the police the absurd idea that there was anyone on the premises to whom dear Viola's death would be a real benediction. It would be most unkind. It would be such bad publicity for dear little Molly. We've outgrown that sort of thing, these days. In these days scandal is Hollywood's kiss of death."

"If I hear that again, or read it again, Eustace, I'm going to begin not to believe it," I said. "There's a line you'd probably call corn . . . 'The lady doth protest too much . . .'"

"It's box office, darling. We have to be realistic about a lot of things."

Tottering down the narrow winding cement road on high heels, long shining cars streaking silently around the curves blinded with high hedges and high walls, I thought another lady would have been better advised if she'd been a little realistic herself and waited for a taxicab. Righteous indignation is all right, but its box office is usually bad. By the time I'd lost my way half a dozen times and quite by accident found that enchanting little spot, the Bel Air Hotel, I was ready to drop. It didn't help much that one of the sleek gleaming leviathans that whizzed past me, missing me by miraculous inches, contained the rotundity of my recent host. A white hand fluttered at me, Stinky Sype squinted his face up in a vanishing smile.

I was furious, first because clopping along the road I knew I was a ridiculous figure, and second because I knew he was out to catch up with Molly McShane. He must have changed from his Chinese get-up with extraordinary speed. And he had to see her. He had to see her before she saw Sheep and Bill and while she was still storm-torn and wretchedly unhappy, in order to frighten her into deeper submission and at the same time re-establish himself in his Tartuffe rôle of sympathetic friend. I was sure that was what was already in his mind when he said he was using his own car but he'd call me a taxi. He wouldn't have whizzed past me on the road we both were going on if it had been anything else.

And he hadn't arrived at the Casa del Flores when I got there over an hour later. Nor had Molly McShane. The uniformed attendant who let me out of the taxi had seen neither of them. But he had seen Bill. He volunteered that.

"I guess he's scared you'll get lost in the wide open spaces, Mrs. Latham," he said.

I went along, to discover further that the grim departure of the girl from Seattle to a soberer, better land seemed to have had no visible effect on the lighthearted cordiality of the staff of the Casa del Flores. My first-born was coming up the stone steps from Viola Kersey's cottage, carrying a chromium food warmer in one hand, a table loaded with dirty dishes balanced on his shoulder with the other. He was whistling cheerfully, as gay as a lark.

"Hiya, Ma! Where've you been?"

I expect I presented a somber note in the happy scene. His grin disappeared at once.

"What's the matter? Something wrong?"

I shook my head. If things had been much worse I would still have loved him at the moment . . . for his resilience to the depression he and Sheep had been in the night before, and for the cocktail sauce that was dripping down the table onto the shoulder of his white starched coat . . . and for the poignant knowledge I had that he didn't yet have.

"Nothing, sweetie," I said. "If you'll bring me some coffee, or something, I'd like to talk to you."

"Okay, Ma. Coming up."

"And you're spilling stuff, baby," I said.

He grinned cheerfully and tilted the table level.

"People shouldn't eat so much. Mrs. Kersey spends the dough like she had it, all right. She threw 'em the works. Old Gee Gee ate oysters, stuffed squab Amandine, and crêpes suzettes. He'll be back on worse than rabbit food tonight. I'll see you, Ma."

I unlocked my door, closed it behind me and stood there wondering. After the morning's scene between George Gannon and his former wife I could understand the stuffed squab only if the Amandine exuded a slight but unmistakably bitter odor. And I'd have expected her to be eating it at his invitation instead of vice versa. I also wondered who the rest of them were that she was throwing the works to. It was evident that when Mrs. Kersey moved in she moved fast, with none of the deliberate rhythmic grace that characterized her personal locomotion. But there was one person I knew wasn't there at her luncheon, and as she was the center of Mrs. Kersey's scheme of things it could only mean that whatever Molly McShane thought or felt was of no importance whatsoever.

It merely confirmed what had been already very adequately proved in that Peke-infested room in Bel Air . . . a diamond bracelet wasn't worth it, neither was a piece of hemp cord. Somehow I had the feeling that the girl from Seattle wouldn't like it to be that way. If she didn't want some screwy dame accusing her of lifting her crown jewels, she would want even less for some other screwy dame to use her death as an instrument of refined torture under the guise of kindness and generosity. I don't believe in ghosts, but I could almost see her standing there in my patio window, saying "See? Didn't I tell you? I know these dames down here."

It may be fantastic and there's probably no truth in it, and the reason I went directly across the room to the telephone and put in a long distance call to Washington was entirely different and had nothing to do with the girl from Seattle. I only know I felt so then. I felt her presence so strongly that I looked back at the window to see if she was there. I know it sounds crazy, but that's the way it was. And at the risk of being thought a complete psychopath I'll go on with the rest of it.

It was just as I turned and looked for her there in the window that it happened. It was as sudden and as positive an awareness of truth as if she actually was there and was actually on her Bible oath telling it to me. I knew George Gannon was lying. The girl from Seattle had never been on his patio. She came from Mrs. Ansell's to mine, stayed there asleep on the chaise longue until Sheep left. I opened the window. George Gannon was not telling the truth. He was making up a story because Viola Kersey knew there was a woman in his room and he didn't want the population from Maine to Florida to know about it.

And I suppose I should go on and say that as that truth was communicated to me I heard the sweetly far-off crash of fairy cymbals and sudden laughter coming from the wings. But that would be false. All I heard was the ringing of the telephone, and I picked it up to take my Washington call.

"Hello," I said, and yanked the receiver from my ear. The far-off crash of fairy cymbals indeed . . . it was the ear-splitting crash of those iron-bound lungs on P Street in Georgetown. It was the first time I'd ever talked to Sergeant Phineas T. Buck long distance, and apparently he hadn't yet heard of the invention of sound-conduction via rubber-insulated copper wire. I could have heard him without it.

"This is Grace Latham, Sergeant Buck," I said, quietly. "May I speak to Colonel Primrose?"

"The Colonel ain't in, ma'am."

I could see the lantern jaw, and the words coming out of one side of that fissure in the granite fastness.

"Oh, dear," I said. "Where is he? I need him."

It was a humiliating admission to have to make to Sergeant Buck. I could also practically see him turn from the phone and spit over his shoulder, or figuratively, anyway, because I believe he is adequately housebroken and wouldn't think of defiling the Colonel's premises no matter what the provocation. He'd wait, no doubt, till he'd hung up the phone and gone out to the back yard.

"I'll tell the Colonel, ma'am."

It had an effect as depressing as one of Sergeant Buck's own pallburiers—to use an expression of his—and as I hung up I had no slightest conviction he'd even so much as mention it to the Colonel. And even if by any remote chance he'd let Colonel Primrose come to me, he'd probably rather see him dead than on the loose in Hollywood. I've often felt that not even Sergeant Buck could have developed such an ingrained habit of protection without a lot of background of experience. I'm afraid Colonel Primrose must once have been a rake of the first water. Nevertheless, I'd have liked to talk to him. It's one of the encouraging things about rakes. After they've sowed and garnered their last crop of wild oats they have a storehouse full of experience—in some cases—that's denied to the more circumspect of mortals, and the wisdom that comes from it. I could have used some of Colonel Primrose's, just then.

I turned away from the phone, pretty low in my mind. The sound of buoyant footsteps and the tinkling of ice and silver outside that announced the arrival of the waiter, my son, did little to raise it.

He wasn't alone. Sheep Clarke was with him. I could hear Sheep's voice as they stopped outside the door, talking in low excited tones. I thought, "They've got the news." Sheep wouldn't have cut his lab and come from Pasadena as early as this for a conference with Bill unless something important had happened. And I was right about that . . . right, and also very wrong. It was evident the minute they appeared inside the door. The world was theirs and they were on the tipmost top of it. They were beaming, Sheep's freckled face creased in a veritable cobweb of delight, Bill's stretched in a grin that reached from one flappy ear to the other.

"Oh boy! Oh, baby! Oh, Ma!" He put his tray down and whirled me around. "Oh, boy! We've hit it! We've hit the jackpot, Ma!"

Then he and Sheep began to pummel one another and spar, in the inexplicable fashion of the young extrovert male, and bear cubs, and half-grown dogs, going through the motions of combat to show how pleased they are with themselves and each other.

"We've got good news, Mrs. Latham," Sheep said, subsiding first. "Our agent's come through. The dream boat's on her way. He's pulled off a deal."

"You . . . don't mean Eustace Sype, do you?" I asked.

"Right. He called me up. He's as excited as we are. He's——"

"What's the deal he's pulled off, Sheep?"

I must have sounded like the skeleton in armor, or at the least a bucket of ice water, but they were too elated to pay any attention to their elders and betters.

"He didn't go into it—he didn't have time. But he says it's a honey, just what we've been waiting for. He's going to tell us tonight. He says it's the works. And he's our boy. He's all hopped up about it, so baby, it must be good. Come on, Bill—let's go find Moll."

Their exuberance was such that nothing I could have said to dampen it would have had much effect. They wouldn't have listened, or have believed if they had listened. They didn't stop long enough to listen anyway; they were off and away. The young are blind, Mrs. Kersey had said. These were deaf as well as blind. And pretty dumb, I thought. But it was their problem, not mine. I told myself that, aware that I was merely condoning my own cowardice. I could have made them listen if I'd wanted to. It was cowardice, not wanting to see them when they got their jolt, not wanting to be the one that gave it to them . . . or even not wanting to sow any seeds that Eustace Sype could take and feed and water into a flourishing garden of resentment against maternal interference in their lives and plans.

Let Molly tell them, I thought. They'd believe her. If they ever decide to combine Mother's Day and Father's Day and make it Parents' Day, Cassandra is made to order for the patron saint. Whoever wrote first about her no doubt got the idea for her at his mother's knee.

CHAPTER FIFTEEN

THE ROOM seemed suddenly oppressive, and I unlatched the screen and stepped out onto the patio. It was cool and quiet and pleasant there, with the last shafts of sunlight shooting luminous filmy planes across the rim of the Canyon above me. I stood looking up at the rugged wall that formed a shadowy friendly fortress around us.

A clicking sound like the one a hedge-clipper makes came from the terrace below me, and I moved over to the rail to look down. Along the path that made the back entrance to my patio, Mrs. Ansell's and George Gannon's was a brilliant border of yellow and bronze chrysanthemums against a mass of some heavy-leafed vine that covered the low retaining wall down to the next level. A woman with a basket was cutting flowers. It was the sound of her shears that I'd heard. She was bending over, absorbed in her task. It was the way she turned her head that caught my attention just as I started to go back inside. I didn't go. I stayed and watched her.

The woman was Rose Shavin, the night maid of the Casa del Flores, Molly McShane's mother, and her gaunt figure bending over, cutting the yellow and bronze sprays, was engaged in a deceptively simple way. She was cutting flowers, but she was cutting something else. It was the stout hemp string staked in front of the chrysanthemums to hold them up. She snipped it off, let it lie on the ground until she reached the next stake, snipped again, drew the slack quickly into a ball and dropped it into her basket. She worked quietly and fast. When she reached the end of the border it was not apparent that anything in particular had happened. The plants still stood fairly erect.

There was only one section where they had dropped and were falling over under the weight of the golden heads that nobody had cut before their supporting cord had been removed. That was a section at the foot of George Gannon's staircase. It was just about long enough to reach across another stone staircase, with plenty of loop around two iron rails, tied tightly for someone who had to go down that way returning to 31-B.

I watched Rose disappear at the end of the border. I thought she'd gone, but she came back. She had a ball of used dirty white cord in her hand, and she was looping it from stake to stake, quickly and skilfully and with no pretense of doing anything else. She got to the end by George Gannon's steps where the topheavy plants had fallen forward. She bound them up, looped the string back and tied it. Then she straightened up and stood looking back at the job she'd done. She wasn't more than ten feet down, and maybe as much further toward George Gannon's steps, and I could hear her breathe. It was slow, long drawn, asthmatic, drawn and released and drawn again—the breathing of a woman laboring under tense nervous strain as well as physical exertion. It was a breath I'd heard before, at the end of an otherwise silent telephone wire . . . when Rose Shavin and Molly McShane thought I was Mrs. Viola Van Zant Kersey.

It had seemed a sinister sound to me then. Now? I didn't know. It was hard to say, because I could also see her gaunt forceful body and rigid determined shoulders that had borne their heavy burdens. They were moving now, up and down as she drew her breath and exhaled it again. Then she shifted her basket of flowers to her right arm, and plodded patiently and without haste back the way she had come. She was a gaunt, dour woman. She was patient and plodding. Somehow I didn't think Rose Shavin was through with Viola Kersey yet.

I heard a car at the end gate. The engine started up, coughed and died, and started up again. The car rattled off, its tinny echo lasting several moments. I looked down at the border of the chrysanthemums. The dirty white cord was hidden under the lush foliage and golden blooms. No one could have guessed, looking at them, that they were any different from what they had been.

I turned and went back into my room. It sounds strange, I suppose, but I was glad I hadn't got hold of Colonel John Primrose. In fact, I was very glad. Remembering the woman ruthlessly and relentlessly saying to her child, "You must go," I still remembered her trembling hands, and I was glad, now, that I couldn't get Colonel Primrose.

As I crossed the room to see what sort of stuff it was on the tray my waiter-son had left me, the phone rang. I answered it.

"Hello, Mrs. Latham."

My heart skipped a beat—or maybe two. And he was aware of it, across the whole continent. I heard his warm amused laugh.

"Buck's a lying scoundrel, of course—but he tells me you've finally admitted you need me. I didn't take much stock in it, but I thought I'd better check to make sure."

"It . . . was a moment of weakness, Colonel Primrose," I said. "I'm all over it, now. Everything's fine. You don't have to worry."

"I'm glad to hear it."

I had the impression that he sounded dubious—which he promptly confirmed.

"I was afraid I did have to worry. In fact, I'm not sure I don't, Mrs. Latham. So what about having dinner with me tonight?"

I caught my breath. "Colonel Primrose . . . your Sergeant didn't tell you. I'm in Los Angeles, California."

"So am I." Colonel Primrose was amused again. "I knew you'd get into something. So, dinner, in about an hour. It'll take me that long to get out from the Sheriff's office. I've just been discussing you with Captain Crawford. Will an hour do?"

There was silence from Mrs. Latham. Complete silence.

"One of the pleasant things about you," he went on, patiently and with a kind of devastating evenness, "is that you're entirely predictable simply because you never learn. I've told you before, and I'm telling you again, that people who murder other people are dangerous to be around. You're a charming woman, my dear, and sometimes you act like an awful fool. Someday it'll be you that doesn't wake up at the foot of some stone steps. Those are terms a first-grader ought to be able to understand—won't you try to see what you can make of them? I'll be out in about an hour. Please don't do anything stupid till I get there. Is that quite clear?"

It was clear, and I told him so. I suppose if I'd had any proper pride I'd have told him a great deal more. As he merely shared what seems to be a fairly universal opinion among my friends and well-wishers, there wasn't much point in arguing it, with Captain Crawford undoubtedly sitting a couple of feet from him in his office in the

Hall of Justice. I couldn't see that I'd been particularly or unusually stupid, but of course he hadn't accused me of that. I was just running true to predictable form. And I had no idea what he thought there was stupid for me to do. Anyway, I didn't have the chance to find out. There was a tap on the door, and Lucille Gannon came in.

"I'm going out of my mind, Grace. I want to see him and he won't see me. I don't see *why* he won't see me. He says he's got too much on his mind."

She was a woman who was distraught and hag-ridden and trying desperately to conceal it. And it was so obvious what she was thinking.

"I tell you, Grace, he's always been *devoted* to her. But even if he hated her . . . the idea of somebody . . . of somebody . . . you know. I mean, it's all so *incredible*. It's so *awful*—doing it that way. I mean——"

"Oh, stop it, Lucille," I said. "Stop it. It's no good. You're just working yourself into something horrible. He couldn't have done it, sweetie. He couldn't possibly. Quit worrying."

I wondered if I was being stupid, saying that. It did relieve her, a little. She sat down, leaned her head on her hand and closed her eyes.

"I wish I'd stayed in Palm Springs. I know he's worried about this deal she's discussing with him. But he's discussed deals before. That can't be the reason he's so disturbed . . ."

"I shouldn't think so. Not if he can eat stuffed squab and crêpes suzette."

She raised her head and looked at me for an instant. Then she broke into the only genuine laughter I'd heard from her that day.

"That I don't believe, Grace. If he ate squab and crêpes suzette I know he tried to murder her. Or if he didn't he's going to. You don't know my Gee Gee. The stuff he eats would make a rabbit feel like a carnivore."

The merriment faded out of her eyes and voice as suddenly as it had come in.

"But I do wish he'd see me, Grace. There's something on his mind." She got up abruptly. "They'd have to *prove* it, wouldn't they? It wouldn't be enough if just somebody like . . . well, say like Eustace for instance . . . If Eustace said he saw him, that . . .

that wouldn't be enough, would it? —Oh, don't, Grace! Don't look like that! What on earth's the matter?"

I suppose I did look as horrified as I truly felt.

"Don't you see, Lucille? Don't you see what you're saying? You're practically accusing——"

"Oh, not me, Grace—it's Eustace that might. That's what I'm afraid of. I've been trying to get hold of him all afternoon. I'm frantic about it. I've phoned the house a hundred times and nobody answers. What's he *doing!* Is he with the police, or——"

She broke off with a little gesture of despair. I didn't feel it was my job to tell her that Eustace couldn't answer the phone because he was out somewhere with Molly . . . and still less that one of his servants couldn't answer it because she was at the Casa del Flores clipping the string off the chrysanthemums that bordered the path to George Gannon's secluded patio.

"It's all so dreadful. If Eustace——"

"Lucille," I said. "Stop it. You don't know what you're saying——"

"But just to you, Grace. You're the only friend I've got that I can talk to. You wouldn't repeat anything."

"Not on purpose, of course," I said. "But Colonel Primrose is coming . . ."

"Colonel Primrose? Oh good. That's fine. I know him. I've known him all my life. He'd never let me down."

Which proved—and I could have told her *that*—how little she knew Colonel Primrose.

"You just leave him to me."

She turned quickly to the door. There was someone outside, in the hall. Her hand flew to her throat as she caught her breath and held it for a moment.

"My God!" she whispered. "You don't . . . you don't think anybody heard . . ."

"I don't know," I said. "These walls are awfully thin. Maybe we'd better see."

I went over to the door and opened it. There was no one there. The hall between my room and George Gannon's was empty. It may have been only a trick of the fading light, or of my own disordered imagination, that made me think I saw the last silent movement of George Gannon's door closing. I turned back to Lucille. She was grey as putty, her hand still clutching at her throat.

CHAPTER SIXTEEN

"If he heard me, Grace!"

George Gannon couldn't have heard that, anyway, because I could scarcely hear it myself. She reached forward and steadied herself against the back of a chair.

"I see what you mean," I said. "I don't think the average man would like it very much, whether it was true or false. And if Mrs. Ansell's at home and her closet door is open, she's heard it all too. Doesn't one of the local papers pay one hundred dollars for a hot news tip?"

"Oh, please don't . . . I can't stand it!"

It wasn't either Mrs. Ansell or the paper getting a hot tip that made her so desperate. She didn't even turn to look at Mrs. Ansell's door when I pointed to it. She was focused entirely across the hall.

"I'm frightened, Grace. That house . . . it's so big, the grounds are so big . . . the servants are out over the garage. If he heard me . . ."

I could see what she meant again. And I didn't blame her. If she truly thought her husband had tried to murder Viola Kersey and whether he had or not, she could very reasonably feel alarmed at being alone in a big house that he had equal access to. Guilty or not guilty, I don't know which would be the worse state from which to hear your wife telling a friend she thought you were. I could imagine the impulse to strangle her being strong in either case. Indeed, if George Gannon was guilty, which I found it difficult to believe, it would seem to me Lucille might easily have signed her own death warrant . . . and Eustace Sype's.

It could, of course, have occurred to a first-grader that she'd also, in that case, signed mine, which was more immediately important to me. As it didn't occur to me, possibly Colonel Primrose was justified in his estimate of my mental age. It was Lucille I was worried about, not Eustace and not myself. Granted she was an hysterical fool, she wasn't more of one than any woman would be in her position. It can't be very reassuring to think your husband goes around rigging up booby traps in the dark of the night for people he doesn't care much about. Household accidents are too frequent at best. Except that I still couldn't see George Gannon doing it that way— not from what he'd looked and sounded like during our encounter that morning. It is only fair to admit, however, that my batting average in the crystal ball league is zero point zero.

"I'd just pull up my socks and go on over and talk to him, if I were you, Lucille," I said. "Knock on the door. He'll let you in. He lets a lot of other people in."

She shook her head. "It's a rule we made when we were first married. When he leaves home to work I never interrupt him."

"All right," I said. "If he finds you in a psychopathic ward when he comes out, at least you won't have broken a rule. If he's done any concentrated work the last twenty-four hours he's a genius."

"But he is, Grace. He really is."

We were interrupted just as I started to say "Nuts" or something like it. There was no doubt at all that somebody was outside this time. It sounded like a stampede of wild horses, but it was only Sheep and my son.

"Hi, Lucille!"

They were both still on top of the world. And Lucille did the most instantaneous change of face imaginable. "Hi, Bill—hi, Sheep! How are the gifted amateurs making out?"

She relaxed and smiled at them, a little patronizingly but not too much considering she was a producer's wife.

"Amateurs nothing. We've arrived."

Bill picked up the tray he'd brought me and that I'd not had a chance to do anything about. "Haven't you heard the news? Didn't Ma tell you? Eustace is polishing up the golden wings right now. But I've got to go. I've got an order for a double bicarb with a milk of magnesia chaser."

"Across the hall," Lucille remarked easily. "You'd better hurry. Give him my love, will you?" She turned to Sheep. His lean freckled face was still a cobweb of smiles. "Is this the deal Eustace told me he'd made with my husband and Mrs. Kersey? Is that what you're all so excited about? I can't believe it."

She went over to the table by the patio window and picked up her bag. "I thought you'd hate it. I thought it was a dirty stinking trick to play on . . ."

She stopped abruptly, listening a moment, reached across the table and drew the curtain to one side.

"Bless me, look who's out here. You startled me, dear. Come back . . . we've all seen you now."

Neither Sheep nor I had seen anything, but we saw then. It was Molly. She was still in her scuffed moccasins and white sox, and she'd put on her camel's hair coat but her hair was still slicked back as it had been when she was on her way to class and as it had been at Eustace Sype's. She was pale as a small ghost as she came reluctantly in through the screen Lucille held open for her. Her eyes were pale too. She looked whipped and numb, like the pictures of Europe's unhappy children you see in the papers, and almost as starved as one of them the way her skin clung to her high cheek bones and to her pointed chin.

"Molly! Baby, what's the matter?"

Sheep made a dive across the room to her. "What's wrong, honey?"

She edged away from him, stepping aside so the coffee table was between them.

"She's sold out and she didn't want to be the one to break the news," Lucille Gannon answered for her—unpleasantly, and with a laugh that didn't make it any pleasanter. "Nothing like eavesdropping to get the real dope, is there, Molly?"

It must have been Molly we'd heard on the patio, instead of someone in the hall, I thought quickly, aware that Lucille was thinking the same thing.

"—Why don't you be honest for once? Why don't you tell Sheep you've sold out to——"

"That's enough, Lucille." Sheep turned to her, his face hard.

She shrugged. "Ask her. There she is. Why don't you ask her?"

"Molly—what is it?"

He turned slowly back to her. "Come on, honey. Don't be this way, Moll."

Her face turned up to his was helplessly revealing for a moment, before she lowered her long dark lashes and nodded her head. She moistened her lips.

"I've sold out, Sheep. She knows. Ask her."

Her voice was dark and softly vibrant. I thought for an instant it was me she meant, but it was Lucille. The bitter lines at the ends of Lucille's mouth were as deep again as if they'd been cut there, but fire was glinting in her eyes.

"I don't know what you mean by that, Molly," she said sharply. "All I know is what your friend Eustace Sype told me this morning— that you're going to live with Viola Kersey, to repay an old debt, and that it's superb for you because you'll have furs and jewels and clothes and cars. Viola Kersey is taking you over. That's all I know. And she's putting up the money for a picture she thinks you'll star in. If you mean anything else you'd better explain."

"That's all I meant," Molly said quietly. "What else is there for me to mean, Lucille?"

"It depends on how long you've been eavesdropping. It's a habit some servants——"

"I told you that was enough, Lucille." Sheep's deliberate tone was deadly. "Now I'm telling you to shut up, and get out."

She put her bag under her arm and moved a step or two toward the door. She stopped there and turned, her dark pencilled brows arched a little.

"Of course, it's none of my business, Sheep," she said lightly. "But aren't you and Bill cutting bait, yourselves? When you talked to me about all this silly business of guardianship, you said if worst came to worst one of you might have to marry her. You've changed your minds about that, have you?"

I've said I thought Lucille Gannon was a fool. She was either more of one than I'd thought or one with an amazing amount of courage. The cold blue devils burning in Sheep's eyes and the set of his jaw and the hard thin slash of his mouth were things she faced cool and unruffled that I wouldn't have cared to face at all. Or it could have been sheer effrontery.

There was a dangerous and grimly silent moment. Then Sheep said, "No. We haven't changed our minds."

"All right, then. Why don't you marry one of them, Molly? If you haven't sold out—if all this *is* against your will—why don't you marry one of them? Or are you just waiting till one of them asks you?"

I would have thought then that Molly would have flamed into the small jungle cat I'd seen the day before. But she didn't. The only evidence of it was a single sidelong look, contemptuous and violent, she cast toward Lucille, and a momentary stiffening of her body. Both stopped as Sheep turned to her.

"Will you marry one of us, Molly?" he asked deliberately.

She shook her head quickly. "No."

It was clear and firm and positive, even though she did not look at him. She was looking at the floor, her pale pointed face set and unyielding.

"Will you marry me, Molly?"

I saw the almost imperceptible quiver tremble across her face. She raised her eyes to him. The pulse in her smooth brown throat throbbed for an instant.

"No, Sheep. Thank you a lot, just the same."

"I want you to marry me."

He started to put his hands out to her, but she moved back quickly.

"No, Sheep. You don't want to marry me, and I won't marry you. She's trying to make you do it—don't you see? She's trying to push you into it. She thinks she'll get rid of me that way. She thinks I want something she's got. But she's wrong. I don't. I just want to be let alone, and I'm not going to let her make anybody marry me just because she wants it that way!"

Lucille was drawing her gloves on with easy, and to my mind, maddening deliberation.

"Oh, you misunderstand me, Molly. It's just that I admire quixotic young men. Why don't you be honest, dear? After all, you've lived here very happily, with your parents doing menial labor to help support——"

"Stop it! Don't you dare speak of my mother that way!"

The little tiger-cat sprang out in full violence then. She flashed around. Sheep stepped between her and Lucille.

"You'd better go." It was I who said it, this time, and just at that moment the phone rang. I knew it was Colonel Primrose, and a wonderful time for him to barge in. But I picked it up. I didn't know whether to be relieved or still more upset when it wasn't the Colonel. It was the girl at the desk.

"Mr. Eustace Sype is in the lobby, Mrs. Latham. He's hunting Sheep. Is he in your room?"

"Yes, he's here. I'll tell him."

I put the phone down. Lucille was at the door, her hand on the knob, waiting. Molly had subsided a little, with Sheep holding her hand. She was quivering, still convulsed with helpless rage. As for Sheep, I didn't know. It hardly seemed the time for him to see Eustace Sype, but there was no way out of it that I could see.

"Eustace is in the lobby to see you," I said.

His big hairy red hand released Molly's abruptly. "Good," he said. He took two long steps toward the door as Lucille pulled it open and stood quickly out of his way. It was a sort of Bombs Away effect over an alert bristling target . . . good, maybe, but I couldn't think good for Eustace Sype.

"Give your fat friend my love, won't you, Sheep." Lucille smiled, as falsely as ever Eustace had done.

"Oh, Sheep, stop! Oh, stop him, Mrs. Latham!"

He went out without a word or a glance back, and slammed the door behind him.

"Let him go, Molly," Lucille said. "It's fish or cut bait. You can't play it both ways at once. Even you ought to know that much."

It was Lucille's parting shot. The door closed again. Molly was across the room in a flash then, tugging at the doorknob.

"Wait, Molly!" I said. "Please wait."

I didn't think she'd hear me, much less obey. But she did. She dropped her hands to her side and turned back to me.

CHAPTER SEVENTEEN

"I GUESS YOU'RE RIGHT," she said simply. "And she's right. It's fish . . . or cut bait."

"It's neither one, Molly," I said. "It's keeping your head, and not letting her goad you into a public scene."

"Goad me . . . that's the word. That's what I was trying to say to Sheep. She's been trying to do it ever since Bill first took me to her house. I don't know why—I don't know why she should hate me like she does. I don't know why after she did everything she could to make the boys think I was a common ordinary floozie she's trying to make one of them marry me now. I think she's crazy."

"I think she's very disturbed," I said. It was a mealy-mouthed thing to say. I don't know why adults always feel they have to ex-

cuse each other to the very clear-sighted young. But Lucille was
an old friend, and even if appeasement has proved a disastrous policy
in maintaining a status quo, I was still trying to work it. "How
long had you been on the patio, Molly?"

She was silent a moment. "I'd just come when Bill and Sheep
came in. I didn't want to see them."

"That isn't the truth, is it, Molly?"

"It's the pragmatic truth." A smile lighted her eyes for a bare
instant. "If that means what I think it means. I mean, so far as I'm
concerned, that's when I came. What I mean is, I didn't hear anything she said about Mr. Gannon because I don't believe it. I think
she was lying. And I think she knows she was lying. But that's none
of my business. I came to see you."

She gripped her hands together, as if there was pain in them that
the pressure could relieve.

"About this afternoon," she said evenly. "I didn't want to tell Bill
and Sheep. I wanted Eustace to tell them. He can make black
sound like white. I . . . I wanted them to think as well of me as
they could. I knew they'd . . . well, one of them would feel he
had to marry me. We've talked about it—before Mrs. Kersey came.
They didn't know it was Mrs. Kersey, but I knew it. I knew her
name, anyway. I didn't know much about her."

"What is it all about, Molly?"

She shook her head. "I can't tell you. Mother says I mustn't
tell. She says it would . . . just make trouble, for people I don't
want to make trouble for. People who've been awfully kind to me."

"You mean your mother and father——"

She looked at me in quick surprise. "Oh, no. How could it
make trouble for them? And it isn't fair for Lucille to talk the way
she does. I didn't want them to work here, or anywhere the way
they do. But Mother wanted it that way. She said they've always
worked and they'd go on, and I'd work, and if I made anything of
myself the way they wanted to, then I'd take care of them. It
was a sort of deal we've always had—because I love them very much,
Mrs. Latham."

That I believed . . . as Lucille would have put it in this Hollywood jargon I knew I would never learn properly. But I did believe
it. It was the one clear and steady light that shone through all of
Molly's volatile and complex simplicity.

"But that isn't the reason I'm going to Mrs. Kersey. It isn't the reason I won't marry Sheep . . . or Bill. I wouldn't marry Bill because . . . well, Bill's different. He expects too much of me. He isn't like Sheep. Sheep doesn't expect anything. He just wants me to be myself. Bill's fun—I don't mean that, and I like him a lot—but he's only thinking about . . . my career. He never thinks about me myself. Sheep's different. A lot of times when I go out with Sheep we don't go to the important places—we just go to a drive-in and have a hamburger and sit there and talk. He doesn't care whether I'm educated or not. I guess he doesn't have the . . . the sort of Junior League standards Bill has, because he knows about girls—from a different angle, if you know what I mean."

I smiled—though she was certainly making a first-rate prig out of my first-born.

"I haven't said it the way I mean it," she said quickly. "It's just that Bill's still sticking to our original deal. And Sheep——"

"—has fallen in love with you. Is that what you mean, Molly?"

She blushed. It's an old-fashioned term, but it's what was happening. A radiance warmed her throat and cheeks and softened her eyes as she looked at me.

"I guess that's what I mean. Bill would be disappointed if I was a flop, but Sheep wouldn't care. He'd say it wasn't my fault. He'd say the hell with it, Hollywood didn't know its own business. You can see, can't you? It isn't that I don't think Bill's swell. It's just that sometimes I get tired showing off, and it's nice to have somebody I can be natural with. I don't know. I guess I'm sort of in love with him too. Mother says we'll both get over it."

She shook her head. "Anyway, I can't disappoint Mother and Dad, after the way they've worked. I don't want to disappoint Bill either. But I've got to take care of Mother and Dad. I've got to do that."

"Can't you do it without going to Mrs. Kersey?" I asked. "Do you want all the things she's going to be able to give you?"

"I don't want any of them. I just have to go. Mother says I have to. But it . . . it won't make any difference in me. That was what Mother was afraid of."

She took hold of the doorknob again. "But that isn't what I wanted to tell you. I wanted to tell you not to tell Bill and Sheep I didn't want to go and Mother made me. That's why I wanted Eustace to see them. But now Lucille's torn it, and they're going to think . . . Well, I guess I'll get over that too. I didn't use to know what Mother meant when she talked about your duty, and doing it no matter what happened, but I guess I do now."

"There are various ideas of what duty is," I said mildly.

"I don't think so. You can always tell duty. It's what you don't want to do—it's what you fight against inside you. Duty's when you realize how it'll hurt other people, and you have to choose between that and what would be easiest for you."

Dear me, I thought. If the remnants of the other post-war flapper and bathtub gin era had imbued their offspring with the beliefs Rose and Morris Shavin had instilled in their child, they woudn't be viewing her contemporaries with such hideous alarm. My own standards seemed horribly debased in terms of hers.

Molly raised her head sharply, listening, drew a quick breath, her eyes widening, and then darted across the room to the patio window. She was too late. Bill was in the door before she could get out.

"Molly! What the hell . . ."

"What the hell what?"

If the spirit behind her words was synthetic, it was convincing.

"What's going on, Molly? What's Lucille . . ."

"Lucille's saying I sold out." She hesitated for a moment, and went on steadily. "She's right, if you want to take it that way. I'm going to live with Mrs. Kersey. She's got money to throw away and she wants to throw it away on me. I'd be . . . I'd be a fool if I didn't grab the chance while I've got it."

Bill stood there, staring at her, speechless. She went on, her face a little pale but her voice steady.

"After all, Bill, you and Sheep didn't expect me to trail along forever, did you? Fun's fun, but you must have realized the first big chance I had to get somewhere I wouldn't stop and ask your permission."

I will say this for my son, that he took it like a man. He stood there, a little recovered from the initial shock, looking at her without a word.

"I've got to have clothes, I've got to see other people, I've got to live where I'm comfortable, I've got to . . ."

"You've said enough, Molly."

He interrupted her quietly. "You don't have to say any more.

It's okay . . . if that's the way you want it. So long. I won't be seeing you."

He went out. The room seemed filled with disappointment and disillusionment, anger and hurt, in a stunned silence that had its center in little Miss Molly McShane. I don't know what she'd expected him to do, but it wasn't that. She closed her mouth and swallowed, and looked at me, her face quite blank.

"Well," she said. Her voice was small and jerky and tight. "I guess that's what I asked for. I . . . well, I guess I won't be seeing you either, Mrs. Latham. And I guess you'll be sort of glad."

"No, Molly," I said. "I won't be glad."

"I guess you will. And I don't blame you—I'd be glad myself. Goodbye, Mrs. Latham."

I heard her moccasins drag a little as she crossed the patio. The iron gate squeaked and clicked shut with a brittle sort of finality behind her. I stood there a moment. Then I took a deep breath. Then I sat down. Lucille Gannon's thinking being twenty-two and staying twenty-two was success seemed to me as bewildering and cockeyed an idea as anyone in his right mind ever advanced. If the choice between twenty-two and one hundred and twenty-two had been offered to me then I would have settled for a cool quiet place in that loveliest of tombs in Charleston's Middleton Gardens, if the Pringle Smiths could bear to let an outlander in.

Or I would have settled for something to eat. I looked at my watch. It was well over the hour Colonel Primrose had given himself and me. Whether I'd done anything stupider than usual in it I couldn't say. It seemed to me I was the passive agent in any action that had gone on. I had the sudden idea that there was one thing I could do, namely talk this over with the maid, Rose, and that I could do what Mrs. Kersey had done. I could call and demand towels and a pitcher of ice cubes to bolster up my sagging jowls. But I decided I'd better wait. That could be the stupid thing he'd warned me about, and a little soap and water was what my face needed just then. I went into the bathroom and turned on the water, but before I had a chance to use it Colonel Primrose came.

Time and distance have a curious relation to each other. Three thousand miles had somehow translated itself into three thousand time units. Even though it had only been four days since I'd seen him in Georgetown, I had the feeling that it had been a very long time. Until he walked in . . . and then I had the feeling that I'd never seen him at all, or at least was only seeing half of him. Sergeant Buck wasn't there. It was a pure conditioned reflex that made my eyes slip past him to the vacancy three steps behind, always before filled with the granite lantern-jawed presence of his guard, philosopher and friend.

CHAPTER EIGHTEEN

"You LOOK LOST without Sergeant Buck," I said. "Why didn't he come?"

He looked taller too, now that his five feet eleven wasn't dwarfed by the reducing contrast of his self-styled "functotum's" six-feet-four of primeval glacial deposit. His black X-ray eyes were just as alive, however, and his smile as amused and affectionately tolerant. I don't know why I put up with anybody who makes me feel like a half-witted setter puppy, unless I'm really like Lucille at heart and pleased with it. It's probably very flattering.

"Buck can't come to Los Angeles."

"Don't tell me there's a woman with a sheriff. Or *do*, please. I can't think of anything I'd like better to hear. Or is it just a sheriff?"

Colonel Primrose smiled. "It's his tenants. He owns a mile or so of these one-story sun-traps you see out here. He's afraid if he sees them he'll have to repair them or lower the rent. So, he prefers to stay away."

I knew Sergeant Buck was well-to-do but I'd never known where it was he'd put away his take from skinning his fellows at various old Army games.

"Anyway, he has work to do," Colonel Primrose said. "Don't tell me you miss him. Though I remember an Angora cat we had once that died of a broken heart when my father got rid of our English bull."

"I guess that's it," I said. "Though I thought I was just being polite asking. He's no friend of mine."

"All right." His face sobered, and he regarded me with a kind of detached summing-up deliberation. "What's happening around here? I met Bill outside, taking cocktails to this Mrs. Kersey I've been hearing about. He's never been one of my hearty admirers, which he inherits from his mother, no doubt, but he's never been quite as abrupt as this before. Belligerent would be a better word. What's the matter?"

"He's probably allergic to the human race at the moment," I said. "I imagine he'll get over it."

Colonel Primrose smiled politely and patiently. "I didn't come out here for any nonsense, Mrs. Latham. It's all right in Washington where I can have Buck keep an eye on you, or have Captain Lamb keep a prowl car alert along P Street. Out here it's different. It's bigger—everything's a long distance from everything else. This place is God's gift to anybody who wants to hit and run. They don't have five unsolved murders in a row because the police are stupid or politicians. It's the geographical set-up, and the crazy lot of people that are attracted here along with the sane ones. You can't predict what they're going to do from minute to minute."

When he stopped I had a chance to say something that had been simmering at low heat from the minute he started. I must have sounded a little like George Gannon, I'm afraid.

"So you didn't come out here for any nonsense, Colonel. I didn't come out here for any more lectures on how stupid I am, or how difficult, or——"

"Not stupid, Mrs. Latham. Difficult certainly . . . but it's your contrary and quixotic inability to mind your own business that I object to. That's all I object to, and when I marry you I'm going to put bars on the windows and——"

"I should think that would settle one problem, then," I said. "And I've been through too many scenes today to help play one. You can ask Bill what's wrong with him. You can go back to Washington. The only thing you can't do is badger me. I'm sick of it."

For some inexplicable reason I was suddenly on the point of tears, and I'm not a weeping woman. I suppose it was the wear and tear of a long day. Anyway I should try it oftener. I'd forgotten what it felt like to be against tobacco-smelling worsted and have my head patted and hear a contrite male voice saying, "There, there. Forgive me, Grace. I didn't mean to upset you, my dear." It was all so absurd that I couldn't help but laugh, and heaven knows I needed to laugh, after the affairs of George Gannon and Viola Kersey, Eustace Sype and the Shavins, to say nothing of Lucille and the three torn and mangled young that I'd been coping with for the last hour and a half.

"I'm hungry," I said. "If you'll go sit down, I'll wash my face."

"That's like a woman . . . you think she's weakened and all she wants is food."

He went and sat down nevertheless, relieved, I suppose, that he wasn't in for a full-blown typhoon. "I'll order us something here. I want to talk to you. I still mean what I said."

I knew he also meant he wanted to see my son. There was one nice thing about him, however, Machiavellian though he might be. He didn't pretend he wanted to dine alone with me on account of my *yeux bleus*. Of course if Sergeant Buck had been there we'd have met in the lobby. The sound of running water in an adjacent bathroom would have curdled Sergeant Buck's blood.

And I tried to think what I'd better tell him—Colonel Primrose, I mean. It depended a lot on what my son would say when he brought our food, and how much he already knew from having spent time with Captain Crawford at the Sheriff's office. What Bill said in words when he came, was not a great deal. The way he said it and the way he looked was revealing. And behind his amiable pretense of composure and utter detachment Colonel Primrose was as alert as a hound dog at a rabbit hole.

I thought my son was just plain sore, rather than belligerent, and I thought he had every right to be. It made him rather more efficient as a waiter than he had been before. He brought the table and the food-warmer in and set them down. Only once, when he took my napkin by one corner and flicked it open and across my lap with a "Will there be anything else, madam?" did he give me anything in the least resembling a wink or a smile, and they were both exceedingly sardonic.

"Where's Sheep, Bill?" I asked.

"I haven't seen him. One of the fellows said he met Eustace in the lobby and went up to his house with him."

"And Molly? I think you're being a little too hard maybe——"

He stiffened abruptly and cut me off.

"She's gone to bed with a headache. Or that's what Rose says. I tried to see her, but no soap. I guess she'll do all right."

He picked up the food-warmer and started to the door. "It's giving Lucille a big kick," he said quietly. "She and Mrs. Kersey are just like that." He held up two fingers to show how close.

"Is she at Mrs. Kersey's now?" Colonel Primrose asked.

"No, sir. She was, but she whipped off up the hill. But she'll be back. They've moved another poor dope out here so she can have her room tonight. Well, I got to go. Are you paying the check, Colonel, or is Ma feeding you?"

Colonel Primrose paid it.

"I'll let you off the tip, sir. I hope we don't draw any more family or friends. And where's old Iron Pants, sir?"

"That isn't polite, dear," Mother said. "Sergeant Buck couldn't come."

I wanted to stop him, quick, before he referred to the Sergeant by any of the other names he and his brother use. He could even make a mistake and call the Colonel to his face some of the things they call him behind his back—The Military Mind being the least offensive of the lot. "How are you and the The Military Mind getting on, Ma? Going to push the fledglings out of the nest and give it to old Catchem and Hangem?" But at the moment Bill was sticking to his formal "sir." He was an unhappy and disillusioned young man, trying hard to cover it up, and sore, sore clear to the roots of his being. I didn't like the hard pallor around his mouth or the way his eyes looked. I couldn't tell whether his bitter resentment extended to include Eustace Sype, because I didn't know what or how much Lucille Gannon had told him. As he hadn't seen Sheep, he might not know Eustace's part in any of it. Somehow, while I hoped Eustace could pour on enough oil of owl's grease to heal their wounded spirits, I rather doubted it.

"I'll be back in half an hour—that time enough?"

Colonel Primrose listened to the sound of his departing feet on the hall tiles, and put down his cocktail glass.

"I've seen Crawford's report," he said. "Now what is all this about Molly McShane and the two boys?"

"Oh, nothing," I said. "Except that they're promoting her. They found her, and decided to make a star out of her. It started as a gag, and they found themselves stuck with it. Now Mrs. Kersey, who seems to have a lot of money, is taking her off their hands."

"And they don't like it?"

"Apparently not."

He smiled at me. "All right. Skip it, if you like. Let's get on to this girl who was killed. I read about your passage with Mrs. Kersey. There was a string, I take it?"

"She said so at first. The autopsy agreed with her, I'm told. But you've read the report. Why ask me?"

"I wondered if you'd thought of anything else, about the other testimony. I feel a little like Mycroft Holmes. There seem to me to be two glaringly simple points in the transcript that may have been overlooked, perhaps because they are so simple."

"What are they?" I asked.

He shook his head. "I'm not Mycroft Holmes. I need more information, not knowing these people. It's a curious situation. Crawford's ostensibly trying to find out who killed this girl, of course. He's more concerned with stopping somebody from trying again to kill Mrs. Kersey. Now, I don't imagine you think there's any sense in thinking Sheep Clarke would feel strongly enough——"

"Sheep Clarke, or Bill," I added for him. "The answer is no. They didn't, at that time, know Mrs. Kersey had any connection with Molly, Colonel. I can assure you of that."

"Then who would you say——"

"Would want to get rid of Mrs. Kersey? Practically everybody around, except Eustace Sype. He's delighted she's here. He says she has a lot of money and he's going to have the pleasure of relieving her of a good deal of it. But how can they assume the girl is so secondary until they know who she is?"

"They do know. They knew as soon as her picture came out in the noon papers."

"Oh," I said. I hadn't seen the noon papers, or the evening papers for that matter. "Who is she? Who was she visiting here?"

Colonel Primrose shook his head. "Nobody. She came here on a date and got stood up. She was an operator in a beauty parlor in Beverly Hills. The woman who manages it called the police, and went down and identified her. She had a date with an actor who's shaking in his bottle-green slacks at this point for fear his name is going to come out. He's doing a period picture and had to have his hair dyed and a permanent wave put in it. The girl did both jobs. His story is that he thought it would be a handsome thing to take her to dinner and give her a big thrill. She was all set up, according to her friends, bought a new dress and a bottle of fancy perfume, got the works at her own shop and left to keep her date here at the hotel."

"And he didn't show?"

"He says he forgot it entirely. Perhaps he did, perhaps he never intended to keep it. Anyway, he spent the evening with one of his ex-wives and some friends at Mocambo. He's absolutely in the clear. A columnist was there to prove it with pictures for the Sunday paper. He and the ex-wife are getting married again. Crawford says it's taken a slight crimp in him, but what he's chiefly worried about is keeping it out of the papers . . . as is his studio."

"And nobody worries much about the girl," I said. "It was a dirty trick. If he'd shown up she wouldn't have got tight and been wandering around . . ."

"And Mrs. Kersey would have got it."

"But it probably wouldn't have killed her. She's got too much padding."

He bent his head down and around, the way he has to from an old wound in the other war, and looked at me, his black eyes contracting the way an excited parrot's contract.

"Well," I protested. "Everybody who falls down steps doesn't die. They may break something, but they don't necessarily die of it."

He looked at me rather oddly. "You're right. Don't you see that's one of the interesting points about it? Nobody could count on her being killed. Either they were stupid, or not actually counting on it—or had some reason to think it would work. If she had a bad heart, for example."

"I don't think she has a heart of any kind."

Colonel Primrose shook his head a little.

"Let me give you some information," he said. "It's a mistake to think the police are fools, or lazier than the rest of us. People forget they have access to a lot of information. They know facts about people. For instance: they know Molly McShane is the daughter of Morris and Rose Shavin, who work here and for Eustace Sype. They know the Shavins were the last servants Mrs. Kersey had when she was Mrs. George Gannon. They know Gannon reported the theft of a diamond bracelet shortly after they left and the Gannons were divorced. He collected his half of the insurance. The insurance people hunted the Shavins down but couldn't find the bracelet. Two months after Viola Gannon became Mrs. Kersey, she repaid the insurance company—Gannon's half as well as hers. The deal she made with them was that Gannon shouldn't be told about it. Kersey was a prominent man, they were glad to settle for cash and shut up. But you can see that a bungling, amateur attempt to injure Mrs. Kersey the day she arrived, when there was known to be a good deal of hard feeling as a result of the bracelet incident, puts the Shavins in a tight spot."

I could see it very well. Moreover, I could see that anything I said would put them in a tighter one.

CHAPTER NINETEEN

WHEN I DIDN'T SAY ANYTHING, Colonel Primrose looked at me with that urbane, patient, cat-amused-at-mouse smile.

"Let's continue, Mrs. Latham," he said blandly. "Has it occurred to you that it might be very much to Mrs. Kersey's interest to have the Shavins in a tight spot, and the tighter the better? Now, her story is that she's anxious to help their daughter. Crawford's impression of her is she's about as likely to want to help anybody at all as a rattlesnake is to help a day-old robin. And so far Crawford's been unable to detect any enthusiasm on the Shavins' part to accept her help. They've been close-mouthed about it, at any rate."

"I think they've accepted it, now," I said.

I thought he was a little surprised.

"They have? When?"

"I don't know that. You'd have to ask them."

"She's the night maid here, on duty now? Call her, will you please?"

I called her, reluctantly and with considerable protest. She came as reluctantly, but nowhere near as volubly protesting. In fact Rose Shavin was grimly tight-lipped. I couldn't tell whether it was fear or a deep-seated antagonism directed at me that made her so sullen and close-mouthed when she came in and found Colonel Primrose there and I explained who he was. She closed the door and stood in front of us, refusing the chair Colonel Primrose offered her. Then she looked at me, plainly taking it for granted I'd told him every-thing I knew and probably a lot I didn't.

"We never intended bothering you, madam," she said at once. "Nobody thought to harm you or frighten you away. It was her we were after. My daughter made a mistake."

Colonel Primrose's black eyes were sparkling at that, I knew, though I didn't look at him. I could feel his satisfaction in the air.

"We wanted her to let our little girl alone."

"And I understand you've changed your mind, Mrs. Shavin," Colonel Primrose said.

She turned from me to him. "Yes. We have."

"Why, may I ask?"

"It's best for our girl."

She used the term very differently from the way Sheep and Bill used it. When they called Molly "our girl" they were amused and affectionate and proud. Rose's use of it had a ruthless and relentless quality, a kind of grim "Spare the rod and spoil the child." I could understand her teaching Molly that duty and desire were categorical opposites.

"Why do you think it is best?"

"Because it is," Rose said stubbornly. "We don't think about anything else. We didn't know Mrs. Kersey had money, we didn't know what she wanted to do for Molly. Now we know it's all differ-ent. The boys have been kind, but they'll get tired of giving out without any return. It's a game with them. It's serious with us. Molly has a right to be a star. She's got it in her. We do what is best for her."

She was as motionless and impassive as a European peasant woman, standing there.

Colonel Primrose got up and moved over to the fireplace. He stood watching her intently without seeming to be more than casually interested.

"When did you decide you wanted to come to Hollywood, Mrs. Shavin?"

She was silent for a moment, her thought processes as slow and plodding, I supposed, as her steps had been down the terrace walk.

"From the day she was born," she said at last. "God gave her to us in our middle age, when we'd lost hope of having a child to love and work for. We'd both been in service out here. We knew it was a place where there was opportunity for a girl no matter where she came from. She almost never cried, like the other girls— she was always laughing, and she danced before she could walk. She made the two rooms we lived in like a big house full of sunshine. It was in Galveston, you can look in the court records. The place not fit for human beings to live in, and she made it happy and good for us from the day she was born. We'd do anything for her, sir."

Colonel Primrose watched her silently for a moment.

"I would be glad to help you do something for her," he said then. "So I'm going to ask you this question. You wouldn't steal a diamond bracelet for her, would you, Mrs. Shavin?"

If you've ever picked up a mud terrapin marauding the strawberry patch and seen it draw in its small angry head and become an apparently lifeless shell, you have some idea of the way the woman withdrew into herself. A hard impervious surface was all that was left of her.

"I think that needs to be answered, Mrs. Shavin," Colonel Primrose said quietly.

Her eyes lighted up slowly with sullen fire.

"I'll answer it. I would. But I didn't. It's a lie if anybody says I stole it."

"In a photograph the police have, your daughter is wearing a diamond bracelet, Mrs. Shavin. Where——"

"I gave it to her. It was mine. She told him I stole it. The insurance detectives came, but I buried it. I knew I couldn't prove I had a right to it, and she'd lie her own mother into the grave. I kept it buried till she paid back the insurance money they got for it. I kept it so my girl would have something when she came here. I'd worked for it. She never paid us for the work we did for her. She borrowed money from us and never paid it back and never told him, and never told him she used the money he gave her for our wages for her own self. She gave us the bracelet and then tried to let the insurance people catch us. She knew nobody would believe what we said against her. She knew we couldn't fight her. You can ask her. She knows it's the truth. She wouldn't dare deny it now."

"And Mr. Gannon . . ." Colonel Primrose began.

"Mr. Gannon is a good man. He doesn't know us now. He

doesn't even look at the maid that comes in his room. Our girl has a part in his picture. If he knew she was ours, he wouldn't be so kind to her, because he thinks we're thieves. We don't want him to know. We asked the police not to tell him."

"Mr. Sype?"

"Mr. Sype knows. He's been very kind to us too. We live at his house, and he pays us well to do the little work we do for him. We didn't want him to pay us, because it's a place Molly can come to and see us. If other people come they think it's because he's her agent that she's there. It works best for Molly."

Colonel Primrose was silent for a moment, his eyes sparkling with some inner satisfaction, derived from what I didn't know.

"One other thing, Mrs. Shavin. How did Mrs. Kersey find out that Molly McShane was your daughter? I understand her real name is Doreen Shavin."

Rose's face hardened, her lips compressed to a thin line.

"We'd like to know, sir."

It was a simple thing to say, but there was nothing simple in its connotation. This was anger, and deep and intense anger.

"She knew as soon as we'd come. She didn't start writing us until three months ago, now—when Molly's first picture came out. It was only a small part, but it showed what she could do. That's when she started to write us. That's when——"

She stopped abruptly, turning her head, and Colonel Primrose swung around at the fireplace.

"Rose! Rose!"

It was Molly's voice, and it came from outside, on the flagstone path between our tripartite cottage and Mrs. Kersey's lush establishment on the terrace below.

"*Rose!*"

It was a frantic cry. All the heaviness and angry lethargy drained out of the woman's stolid body. She was at the french windows with a speed I wouldn't have believed her capable of, and pulled them open. Molly was there, her face pale.

"Oh, Mother, quick! Something's happened! Dad's gone . . . he's gone to Eustace's. And Bill's gone . . ."

"*—Be quiet!*"

"But Mother . . ."

"Be *quiet*, I tell you."

Then there was only Colonel Primrose and me in the room and I was staring at the empty french window where they'd been. I turned and looked at him in a kind of blank alarm.

"Bill . . ."

Colonel Primrose had dropped for once all his amiable composure and all pretense at fine dispassionate objectivity. His face was very grave.

"Get your coat," he said curtly. "Be quick. I have a car outside. Hurry, will you please?"

I was hurrying, as fast as I could. For a moment I was completely distracted. The passionate alarm in Molly's voice vibrated in my ears.

"Those young fools," Colonel Primrose said quietly. "Why do they have to get mixed up with Shavin in this?"

I was too alarmed myself, by now, to ask him what he meant.

"Can't you see what's happening?" he said impatiently. "Shavin's gone up there to Sype's house. It's Sype who put Viola Kersey on the trail of their girl—it couldn't be anybody else. Just try to use your head, won't you, Mrs. Latham?"

He was holding the door open for me.

"And that woman was lying . . . she'd rather be dead than have Viola Kersey take her child."

CHAPTER TWENTY

COLONEL PRIMROSE's car outside the front entrance of the Casa del Flores was one of those long sleek shiny jobs with driver in the glass-partitioned front seat that in Washington, D. C. indicates a diplomat or a funeral. He gave the man Eustace Sype's address.

"I'd like you to make as much speed as you can."

He ran up the glass panel and switched off the communicating instrument.

"I can't make these people out," he said.

Somewhere in the course of our progress between Room 102 and the fancy equipage we now occupied I'd calmed down considerably. Sheep had been at Eustace's too long to have got into any passionate row with him. If Bill had followed him there at once, they could easily have got into a blind rage and beaten the living daylights out of him. That was something I could have viewed with only mild regret, inasmuch as they were hardly likely to bruise their knuckles considering how well Eustace's bones were covered. Nor were they likely to let Morris Shavin do more than give him a formal punch in the nose, which he had coming to him out of ordinary courtesy. I wasn't, thinking it over, too much alarmed. Colonel Primrose could call them young fools, but they were a pretty level-headed pair. Little Morry Shavin could hardly be thought of as savage. Rose would have been a horse of a different color, but neither she nor the little hellcat, her daughter, was there.

"What people?" I asked. "You wouldn't be jumping to any con-clusions? There's a whole theory about everything that doesn't touch the Shavins."

"What are you talking about?"

He was seldom that abrupt with me. I could feel his eyes fixed sharply on me in the dark.

"I'm talking about what happened to the girl from Seattle. I seem to be the only one who ever does. Who killed her . . . even if he was aiming at Viola Kersey?"

"What about it?" His tone was a little more interested.

"Lucille Gannon's sure her husband did it, from all I can make out. She thinks he left Viola in his room, whipped out and down his patio steps, grabbed the cord from the chrysanthemum stakes, tore around to the front, set up the booby trap and got back inside before she missed him. He hops around like a monkey on a string anyway. Maybe he could have done it. She's convinced that if he ate stuffed squab with the lady at her luncheon today he must be planning a second go at it. He usually eats raw garden produce."

"You aren't trying to make me eat a whole red herring at a mouth-ful, Mrs. Latham?"

He sounded like a man irritated but determined to be patient as long as he could.

"That doesn't sound like you. What have you got against poor Lucille now?"

"A lot," I said. "She writes me a frantic letter saying my son's going to hell fast. When I get out here she's in Palm Springs, and she arrives and brushes the whole thing off by saying she got burned up because Bill and Sheep wanted her to do something for Molly.

Establish some kind of guardianship the state law requires for minors working in pictures. She hates Molly with a virulence that doesn't make any sense."

He was silent for an instant. "Are you sure it doesn't?"

"It doesn't make sense for any middle-aged woman to act the way Lucille does about that child," I retorted. "She's really fantastic. If anything happens to Molly you'll know where to look. In fact I'm beginning to wonder anyway. I'll bet she never was in Palm Springs."

"You'd lose," he said. "The police did a routine check on all of you, including Lucille as soon as they found out her husband was staying at the hotel under an assumed name. They phoned her at Palm Springs and got her out of bed, which she wasn't very pleased about. She flew up here this morning and got in at seven-thirty in a private plane that belongs to Jerry de Voe, who's the lead in this picture Gannon's shooting out in the Valley. He flies back and forth because his wife's in their Beverly Hills house until the divorce is final. I thought you were a friend of Lucille's. You surprise me. Furthermore, Mrs. Latham, Lucille has a big stake in keeping Mrs. Kersey alive and well. So has Gannon. He's an independent producer sailing close to the wind. He can use money, and Mrs. Kersey's got it. He'd eat horse meat *au jus* to keep in with her, and so would his wife."

He paused a minute.

"I know Lucille's exasperating——"

"She is indeed," I put in hotly. "She pretends she can't stand Eustace Sype, and I go to see him without warning—at her suggestion —and find they're pals. She's called him up and they've had a cozy chat about how I can be persuaded to help them turn Molly over to Kersey to keep either Bill or Sheep from making a mesalliance."

Colonel Primrose chuckled.

"And she'd already told me about the string over the steps being an original idea of Gee Gee's—straight out of Agatha Christie—so he must have done it, but he couldn't possibly because he adores his former wife. She defeats me. She's the one that told me about the diamond bracelet. I assumed she's burned up about that because Gee Gee didn't get his cut, but if the insurance company paid him——"

"He may not have told her that."

"But it's none of her business. She wasn't married to him then."

"All right, all right," he said. "Relax, my dear. Gannon's interest, and Lucille's, is keeping Viola Kersey alive. Anything either of them says to the contrary is balderdash. Gannon gave Crawford a tirade about it this morning, and he ate stuffed squab with her at lunch. It's an old Hollywood custom, Mrs. Latham. Read the columnists. They're always confirming something they've printed that was denied. It gives double the publicity——"

"You've got Hollywood wrong, Colonel," I said. "They don't like publicity. I get that through the walls from Mrs. Ansell. She's been trying to see Lana Turner for I don't know how long."

He chuckled again. "Then Miss Turner's the exception. She doesn't need publicity, or she doesn't like the story, or she doesn't like Mrs. Ansell, whoever Mrs. Ansell is."

"All right," I said. "Then what is it Lucille's afraid of? Why is she coming to the hotel tonight? Why is she afraid to stay in her big house? She's afraid of somebody."

"Of course she is," Colonel Primrose said. "She's got a little common sense and she values her expensive hide. I wish you were like her. She knows a murderer isn't trustworthy. He has a thousand suspicions that a normal person would reject at once. He can't afford to—he can't afford to take a chance."

He looked out the window. We were passing the lights of the main Bel Air gate.

"I wish I could remember the number of times I've tried to make you see that. You get mixed up in this sort of thing, and you get hold of something you think is perfectly innocent knowledge. You don't even know it is knowledge. The person who has bloodguilt on his soul doesn't think about that. He lives with a dark terror, Mrs. Latham. He isn't likely to stop and ask whether you know the meaning of what you've got. Take the example of what you just said."

"What did I say?"

I'd said far too much, but I couldn't think of anything in particular.

"You said Lucille thinks Gannon whipped out and got the cord off the chrysanthemum stakes. That's dangerous knowledge, my dear. Crawford hasn't got it. They've hunted high and low to find out. And don't think some guilty mind hasn't been watching them. Did Lucille say that?"

"No," I said. "I . . . it just came to my mind. It's just a pure guess."

He drew a deep breath. "I'm really serious about this."

"Do you really think the Shavins set that trap for Viola Kersey?"

I knew I ought to tell him about Rose down at the border of chrysanthemums below the stone steps, but I couldn't bring myself to do it.

He said slowly, "I think Viola Kersey is an actress. It was actually someone else who tripped over the cord, wasn't it?"

I turned and looked at him in the shadowy darkness of the car. We'd turned off Sunset Boulevard and were rounding one of the blind narrow curves on the upward road. I thought it over a moment. It wasn't Viola Kersey who'd tripped.

"But that doesn't make sense, Colonel Primrose."

"Crawford thinks it does."

Our car made a crazy swerve to avoid a low almost lightless monster that zoomed around the curve going as if all the jackals in hell were at its tail. It swerved too, and sped hideously on. It was my son's hot rod, but he wasn't in it. The white glare of our headlights as he swerved through them had thrown Sheep Clarke into ghostly relief just long enough to leave him a vivid after image in my mind. I caught my breath.

"That was Sheep, Colonel."

He grabbed the broadcloth hand loop beside him and pulled himself forward to run down the glass panel between us and the driver.

"Are we about there?"

"Yes, sir. A couple more curves and to the right and that's it."

He speeded up still more. Colonel Primrose sat on the edge of the seat. I was still back in my own corner, still seeing the white set blur of Sheep's intent and urgent face behind the wheel of the hot rod. I was praying he would get wherever he was going, and I was curdled with the fear that he wouldn't . . . not at that rate, not on that road.

Then we were where we were going. The iron gates stood open. Eustace's car was in the drive, sleek and handsome in the box of yellow light from the open front door. There were no dogs yapping. Our own motor and our tires crunching to a stop behind the other car were the only sounds around us. It seemed an almost monstrous silence, magnifying the sound of our door slamming and our footsteps quick across the white sand and up the four steps into the empty hall. And still there were no dogs. The black lacquered doors at the end of the hall were closed, but abruptly one of them opened. It was Bill, and there was surprise on his face, seeing the two of us there. It wasn't us he'd expected to come. It was someone else. It took an appreciable moment for him to speak.

"Come in, Colonel. Mother, you stay there."

I didn't stay there, but I wished I had. Much as I disliked and mistrusted Eustace Sype, I never wanted to see him the way he was then. Or see the shaken cowering figure of Morris Shavin against the door over by the fireplace. He was actually green, as if it took all the physical control he was capable of to keep him from being actively sick. Or see all the little dogs, frozen to immobility, sitting halfway across the room, a lot of small fluffy creatures each studded with a pair of bright anxious waiting eyes.

A sudden impulse made me clap my hands twice.

"Go away, boys and girls!"

It was a dreadful sound in the hideous silence of that fantastic room, but they were waiting for it. They broke and ran pell-mell through the terrace door, not a yap out of them. They ran straight past their master. He was lying face down on the floor, the whole back of his coat a wet red mass.

CHAPTER TWENTY-ONE

"WE TRIED to save him, sir," Bill said quietly. "Sheep's gone for a doctor. But it's too late."

Colonel Primrose was kneeling beside the bloated figure on the floor. He held his fingers to the wrist for an instant.

"Call Captain Crawford, Bill. He can call the city police."

His eyes moved around the room. Bill came over to me.

"Come on. Let's get out."

"I'll stay," I said. "Go and phone."

It wasn't the thing on the floor that had once been Eustace Sype that I was concerned with. It was the other thing . . . the thing in his cherry-red silk cushioned seat. It was a bayonet, sticking up from the back, a gaping hole around it where the silk had torn. It had fallen forward, blood-stained, its point pricked into the silk where it had fallen. Colonel Primrose was standing over it, bending forward, not touching it, putting his hand carefully against the back of the seat, to see how it had done what it had. I remembered seeing Eustace Sype waddle in and stand there, and give his feet that absurd outward thrust that let his grotesque body collapse down into his luxurious throne, with his temple bell and his jade-headed gong on the low Chinese table to his right. I could see him now. He was like Victoria, I'd thought. He didn't have to look to see that his seat was ready behind him. In the dim lights of that exotic room he wouldn't in any case have seen the weapon fixed there, hidden in the heavy silks, and once he'd collapsed down on it he was lost. Whoever had fixed it there knew Eustace Sype. They'd watched him thrust his feet out, as I had. They knew he never looked before he sat there.

Colonel Primrose bent closer down behind the seat. I saw him gingerly lift a small square of the silk, cut around three sides, where the bayonet had been thrust through.

He straightened up, looking at Morris Shavin in his personal and private agony beside the door.

"Are you Shavin?"

The man could only nod, and fumble with shaking hands into his pockets to bring out his papers to show he had a right to live, because he lived in America, not in his native land. He was speechless with despair. Tears were streaming down his cheeks.

"Get a sheet or a blanket and bring it here," Colonel Primrose said. He turned back as the old man stumbled off. "What happened?"

He was speaking to Bill who'd come back—as serious and sober-faced a young man as I've ever seen him be.

"We don't know what happened, sir, any more than you do now," he said steadily. "Sheep was here with him, out in the dining room. They'd been talking. Morry and I came when Eustace was finishing his supper. He sent Morry to get some ice and soda and brought Sheep and me in here. We followed him. He went over to his regular seat here and sat down, and that was it. We thought he'd had a stroke. We called Morry and got him some of his smelling salts. We tired to move him, but we couldn't. He kept making gurgling noises we couldn't understand. Sheep called all the doctors he could around here. One finally said he'd come and to let Eustace alone, but he kept trying to struggle up, and at last the three of us pulled him over. And that's the way it was. The way you see it. Gee, what a way to go. He wasn't a bad guy. He was sort of a screwball, but he wasn't a bad guy."

It was a curious epitaph for Eustace Sype, but as sincere a tribute, I supposed, as he was likely to get.

"Sheep has gone for a doctor?" Colonel Primrose asked quietly. Bill nodded.

"Where did that come from?"

Colonel Primrose was pointing to the blood-stained bayonet sticking out of the torn silk. The white down was stained as red as the cherry covering.

"That's what sort of got us, sir. It's one we gave him. We took it off a dead Jap on Okinawa. I told you, Mother, he was a V. I. P. we towed around. He was a souvenir hound, and we got him a lot of stuff. He's got a collection of it on his wall in there."

He jerked his hand toward the door Morry Shavin had gone through.

"It makes you feel sort of . . . responsible."

"You needn't," Colonel Primrose said briefly. He looked back at the inert thing on the floor. "Where's Shavin gone? I sent him to get a sheet."

"I'll go see, sir."

"There's something burning," I said. "It's paper."

"The damned fool!" Colonel Primrose said bitterly. He was through the door, Bill at his heels. He must have missed his iron leg man, I thought. Sergeant Buck had always hovered behind him, ready to give chase so his superior could stay at the center of things.

It left me alone there, and I moved quickly around to follow them, because I didn't like being left there with Eustace Sype. I had to pass him, and for an awful instant I saw his face. It must have been a trick of the golden salmon-colored lights, but I was so startled that I stopped, staring down at him. It could have been a trick of my own imagination, growing out of the profound distrust I had for him. I saw then that he wasn't smiling. What I'd thought was the shadow of one of his self-satisfied malicious smiles was nothing but the shadow of a face distorted with a paralyzing grimace. It could have been malice, however. Not even death could make Eustace Sype a noble figure. But pity I could feel for him. It seemed the most horrible irony that he'd been defeated, in a way, by his own frustrated and overweening ego. I could almost hear him saying, "I couldn't be the tallest man in the world, so I decided to be the widest." If he'd been content to stay a small man he wouldn't have died . . . not this way.

Colonel Primrose and Bill had gone through the room next to us, a sort of grotesque museum and picture gallery with souvenirs and signed photographs that even whipping through it as fast as I did I could recognize as a Who's Who of Eustace's world. They were in the room past it, a library and study, panelled, with solid leather chairs and nothing of a Chinese-Ottoman empire about it. It was a work room, with filing cabinets behind the pine panels on one side. A door to them was open, one drawer still out. Morris Shavin was there too, by the fireplace. The single gas jet, like a flame-thrower, that they use out there to light the fire was still on, and a mass of charred paper it had consumed was black and powdered under the andirons. Bill had just bent down and was turning the gas off. Shavin was a cowering figure, with Colonel Primrose beside him.

"What did you do it for, man?"

Morris Shavin had found his speech.

"He told me. He showed me the box. He said if I die, you burn it first thing. I trust you. You burn it. He said so."

He kept saying it, pointing to the empty file that had slipped out.

Exasperation is a mild word, I thought, for the acute and futile annoyance with which Colonel Primrose turned away from him. I've seldom heard him swear, and never before under his breath. He went over to the file, pulled it out further and jammed it back in again. Morris Shavin continued an unintelligible babble about Eustace's orders to him until the Colonel finally silenced him.

"That's enough. Try to explain it to the police, with Sype murdered out there. You'll have to talk faster than you're talking now. Call the hotel, Bill, and have Rose sent up here as quick as they can get her here. Then take your mother out and leave her in my car."

That was me he was talking about. When I started to protest he silenced me as curtly as he had poor Morry Shavin.

"Do as you're told, Mrs. Latham. And stay in the car. Don't get out of it, and don't go anywhere until somebody goes with you. You're not in Washington, D.C., and you're in everybody's way. Don't you be a——"

"You brought her here, Colonel. There's no use getting sore at her. Come on, Mother."

There was a quick flicker of a smile in the glance Colonel Prim-rose shot me as my son took hold of his parent's arm to take her out.

"Sorry," he said. "Take her out anyway."

Bill took me out. We went through Eustace's elaborate dining room. The remnants of his supper were on the long black lacquered table that extended almost the entire length of an otherwise snow-white job of interior decoration. The dirty dishes and half-eaten food gave it an air of broken meats in a mausoleum. His chair was pushed back, his fork had fallen on the floor. It looked like a table from which a diner had departed rather hurriedly. One other chair was pushed back, a wine glass tipped over. If Bill hadn't been with me I think I would have straightened it up a little. The sense of abrupt departure didn't look too well, when the finally departed host was so palpably a man who lived to eat. Bill's story had left that angle of it out. I wondered. He'd made it all sound like a casual affair.

"Were you very angry when you came up here?" I asked him as he held the door into the hall open for me.

"I was sore as hell. I got outside after I'd taken your table in, and Lucille was there. She was coming back from getting her overnight bag and she had a flat a couple of hundred yards up the road. She was on her way in to get one of the boys to go change her tire. I don't know why she couldn't change it herself—she's always blowing off about what she did in the Motor Corps during the war. I sup-pose she didn't want to get her gloves dirty. She asked me to go change it and I said the hell with it, I was working. That made her sore, and she started taking cracks at Molly for giving Sheep and me the go-by. I was sore too, I guess. I told her she ought to mind her own business, and she said it was time I was finding out who my friends were. She said, 'Why don't you ask Mrs. Kersey who told her Molly McShane was born Doreen Shavin?'"

He opened the car door for me. The driver was asleep in the front seat, snoring peacefully. Bill got in beside me and ran up the glass panel.

"I said okay, I would."

He pulled the door to quietly and lowered his voice.

"And I did. I went down and asked her point-blank. She gave me a lot of business about dear Lucille's not understanding her interest in her former husband, and all that, and she got sore, too. I seem to rub everybody the wrong way tonight. It seems nobody understands Mrs. Kersey either, or how tenderly her heart beats. Anyway, she finally said okay, if we really wanted to know, it was Eustace Sype. She said he——"

He stopped, listening. "Here they come."

He opened the door, leaned over and gave me a quick kiss on my cheek. "You stay here—*please*, Mamma. Don't want you mixed up in this."

He hadn't got the door banged shut before the courtyard on the rim of the Canyon there was a milling carrefour of squad cars and motorcycles and policemen, in uniform and out. It was like the locusts descending. Somewhere in the distance I heard the dogs yap, but only half-heartedly and only a few times, and then the furry little boys and girls were quiet as mice again. Our driver was awake and a startled man, and he was more startled when a uniformed officer got him out of the car and disappeared with him . . . leaving me alone and completely ignored, with only an occasional bewildered and inquiring face pressed to the window as its owner passed back or forth. If you sit quietly it seems to confuse people. These seemed to take it for granted I had some proper reason for being there and let it go, until Captain Crawford himself came out.

"The Colonel says you're to go back to your hotel, Mrs. Latham," he said. "You're to go back and go to your own room and stay there."

He gave me a bleak smile.

"That's what the man said. You heard what the man said. I'll get your driver for you."

And Sheep hadn't come back. I was thinking of that as we rounded the narrow corner where we'd almost had the head-on collision with him in Bill's hot rod. He couldn't have taken so long to find a doctor. Then I wondered again if he'd piled up somewhere, going at the speed he was going when he passed us. It seems strange to say it, but I was aware that I was choosing that as the lesser of two evils, choosing it to keep from having to doubt that my son's story of Eustace's death was as simply the truth as it had sounded when he told it.

If I allowed myself to doubt its truth . . . but I couldn't allow myself to. If I did I could never believe my son again. I knew it was the truth he told. He and Sheep had followed Eustace Sype into his bizarre and beautiful room, as Bill had said they had. I could close my eyes and see Eustace's white hand fluttering them to a seat, while he did some rapid calculation in an attempt to conciliate and to appease. I could see the yapping tangled mass of ecstatic fur, and Eustace freezing them to immobility—"Quiet, boys and girls!"—before he flipped out his feet and collapsed into his luxurious cushions . . . and was transfixed there, helpless to save himself or be saved.

I believed it for a fact, the way Bill told it . . . and it occurred to me suddenly that the little dogs were a fantastic sort of witness to the truth of it. There could have been no question of violence. The little dogs wouldn't have been sitting so expectantly, waiting their release, unless their master had still dominated the atmosphere as he took his final and horrible descent into his cushions. Sheep was either piled up somewhere beside the road or he'd gone a long way for a doctor. I refused to consider another alternative . . . and I didn't think of his racing straight to Molly. I'd forgotten how important to him she was.

CHAPTER TWENTY-TWO

I WENT directly through the lobby pergola to the path leading to my room, without stopping to see if there were any messages for me at the desk. If I'd stopped, as I normally would have done, I'd have got the one Lucille left for me, and I'd probably—in spite of what the man had said—have gone to her room to see her. It was unfortunate that I didn't. But I wasn't thinking about messages. I went straight along the flagstone path to 102. As I put the key in the lock, George Gannon's door across the tiled hallway opened abruptly.

"Oh, Mrs. Latham!"

It was the milk-and-honey voice of Mrs. Viola Van Zant Kersey and the last person at the Casa del Flores that I was in any mood to talk to at the moment.

"I'm so glad to see you, Mrs. Latham. I've just been paying another visit to my former husband. You'd think I'd be more discreet, wouldn't you?"

"Or more careful," I said, and regretted it instantly. If she didn't remember what had happened the last time she'd paid him a nocturnal visit, it was hardly my business to remind her. She took it very gaily.

She apparently didn't know what had happened to Eustace Sype . . . and that was definitely not my business to tell her.

"I shall look at the steps, my dear."

She laughed. "I'm prepared tonight."

She held out a gold pencil and pressed the end of it. A small but effective ball of white light bobbed about on the floor before she switched it off.

"And I came up really to see you. I wonder if I might come in for a moment? We have so much to talk about, you and I."

"Do we, Mrs. Kersey?"

I couldn't think what it was, myself. But she apparently could. I didn't like the way her plump face settled behind its outer layer of peaches and golden cream. ". . . I think Viola Kersey is an actress. It was actually someone else who tripped over the cord, wasn't it?" As I heard Colonel Primrose's voice saying it again, a slight prickling along my spinal column warned me that I really shouldn't be stupid or a fool.

"We do indeed, Mrs. Latham," she was saying. "Perhaps you'd prefer to come to my apartment."

"No. You can come in here," I said.

I opened the door. One amber shaded table light was on. And curled up in the bamboo chair, fast asleep, was Molly McShane.

"Oh, how sweet!" said Mrs. Kersey.

I looked at her quickly. It was about the phoniest sounding thing I'd heard for a long time, and it struck me, with a not too bright intuitive flash, that Mrs. Kersey already knew Molly was in my room.

I looked at the patio windows. The curtains were drawn across them more carefully than at any time before, and from the warmth in the room I knew they were closed. I suspected they were securely locked also.

I left Mrs. Kersey to shut the door and went over and turned on another light.

"Molly," I said. She stirred and came slowly up out of a really deep slumber before she flashed to sudden wakefulness. She started up, blinking her eyes and shaking her head.

"Oh, I'm sorry. I——"

It was then she saw Mrs. Kersey by the door.

"Oh," she said.

From a relaxed and sleepy child she turned into something as tightly coiled and tautly held as a steel spring. The black pupils of her eyes contracted to pin points in the hyacinth-blue field around them.

"Oh," she said again. "I didn't know . . ."

"I met Mrs. Kersey in the hall, Molly. She wants to talk to me." I didn't say "It was her idea," but I meant to imply it, and hoped I had.

"I'd better go, then."

"I wish you'd stay, dear. I want to talk to you too."

Whoever had taught Viola Kersey how to place her voice so that it oozed the syrupy mixture it did had done a good job if that is what one likes. Its contrast with the salt and acid quality of Molly's was extraordinary.

"I don't want to hear you talk, Mrs. Kersey."

" 'Vi,' you were going to call me, dear. Or 'Aunt Vi,' if you'd rather. Remember? Didn't Eustace say he thought that would be a nice thing for you to call me?"

Molly's pointed little face went a shade or two paler.

"I told him I'd call you Mrs. Kersey. If that doesn't suit you I can't help it."

"She's so spirited, isn't she, Mrs. Latham? I adore spirit in people. It shows such inner fire. Divine fire on the altar of the soul, I sometimes call it."

I glanced at Molly, shaking my head. She tossed her shining mane back from her face and picked up her bag.

"I'm going," she said curtly.

Mrs. Kersey blocked the door. Her plump, fine figure garbed in black and red flowered print on white ground looked massive to me . . . too formidable for even Molly to storm past.

"I want to talk to you whether you want to, or not." She spoke with what I thought an enforced calm. "I am afraid I lost my temper with Bill this afternoon. I'm sorry for it. I've intended calling Eustace to tell him I was too hasty, but I've been busy."

Molly flashed me a startled inquiry. I shook my head again, quickly, this time. I wanted to know what Mrs. Kersey had to say before she became aware that she didn't have anything to say at all.

"I felt Eustace had been very unjust to me," she said earnestly. "I don't see why I should have to bear the *whole* brunt of this ingratitude. I came wanting to help. It was Eustace who wrote me that my old servants had come to Hollywood."

"But you didn't want to help them, did you, Mrs. Kersey?"

Molly emphasized the "Mrs. Kersey" just enough to make it plain. "You didn't come rushing out to help your old servants then, did you?"

"My dear child." Mrs. Kersey threw her white glittering hands up in despair. "You don't understand. I didn't *believe* Eustace. He's so malicious. I thought he was joking."

"That isn't true and you know it, Mrs. Kersey." The girl was amazingly in control of herself, after the various cyclonic sessions I'd had with her. "Eustace told me that himself, and he has your letters to him to prove it. You waited till you saw my first picture. You wouldn't believe him when he told you I had a chance of getting somewhere. You said you'd wait, and he was the one that had the picture sent you for a private showing before it was ever released. He told me all this. He told me so I wouldn't make the mistake of feeling any gratitude toward you. He was afraid I might. He didn't know me, but he wanted to be sure."

"I know," Viola Kersey said. "He's a dreadful wicked wretch, isn't he?"

Seething inside as I imagined she was, she still had her fortress of honey and caramel intact.

"He has such a quaint sense of humor. Some day it's going to get him into serious trouble."

Molly McShane shook her head.

"No, Mrs. Kersey. Eustace has been in all the trouble he's ever going to be in."

"You children!" If she had listened to the quality of Molly's voice she would not have laughed so airily. "You think you can make Eustace see the error of his ways and turn to righteousness. You underestimate dear Eustace's capacity for malice. You're all exceedingly naive——"

"Mrs. Kersey . . . Eustace is dead," Molly said deliberately. "Eustace was murdered . . . this evening . . ."

"You're lying!"

Then Mrs. Kersey clamped her lips shut, her blue eyes distended, the pulse beating a violent tattoo in her white throat. She flicked her tongue across her lips.

"You're lying!" she cried again. "Mrs. Latham!" She steadied herself against the door. "Tell me she's lying!"

I shook my head. I'd never been around so many people who called each other liars with such unadulterated unambiguity before.

"It's true, Mrs. Kersey."

She kept her eyes on me a long time, but they weren't seeing me. They were seeing something visible only to them. Or seeing nothing. I don't know. The blue-white eyeballs were strained and they had tiny threads of red in them that had not been there before.

Then very slowly Mrs. Kersey moved them, without moving her head, until they were fixed on Molly . . . fixed, and as damnably accusing as if she were pointing her finger and saying it in so many words. It was as plain to Molly as to me what she was thinking—what it was she was saying.

"It's you that's lying, Mrs. Kersey."

Molly's voice was low and passionately intense.

"My parents didn't kill him. That's what you want to think. That's what you want everybody to think. It's a wicked, horrible lie. Mother doesn't even know it was Eustace that told you. Dad knew it, but he kept it to himself because he didn't want her to know. You tried to make her believe Dad had put the string across the steps— but Dad wouldn't do that. He's too kind and too sweet. You don't understand kindness, but he does. He doesn't even hate you, like Mother and I do. He doesn't know *how* to hate anybody."

She flashed away from the woman at the door.

"Mrs. Latham—Sheep brought me down here. He said I was to stay here so nobody could find me. He was afraid for me to stay up in my room alone, with Mother and Dad and Bill all gone, and he had to go back to the house. He took Mother with him so Dad would have somebody who could talk for him when they got him all mixed up. I told him I'd stay, if you'd let me when you came back. But I won't stay if she's going to stay here. I won't——"

"Mrs. Kersey is going, Molly," I said. "Right away. I'm sure she doesn't want to stay."

CHAPTER TWENTY-THREE

THAT WASN'T TRUE. Mrs. Kersey wanted very much to stay. She didn't want to go down those stone steps to the empty magnificence of her apartment. I can't say I very much blamed her, but I didn't want her in mine.

As she moved uneasily, sought of fumbling for the doorknob behind her, I felt sorry for her all of a sudden.

"Wouldn't you like me to go ask Mr. Gannon to go down to your apartment with you?" I said.

She licked her lips again, a kind of new terror on her. Mrs. Kersey was beginning to shake violently. If I didn't get Mr. Gannon, and quick, I thought, I'd have to go myself, and that I didn't care to do. I may say I quite definitely did not.

I looked at Molly. If she had either pity or compassion in her hot little heart there wasn't enough to waste on Viola Kersey. Her head was raised, her chin thrust out a little, no emotion visible in any line of her slim body except contempt of a very high order. Molly didn't like Mrs. Viola Kersey reduced to quivering pulp any better than she liked her opulent sugar and spice.

"Would you like me to get Mr. Gannon?" I repeated.

It was only then that it struck me that if Lucille should happen to be right, I was little better than an accessory before the fact. But he was all there was. She seemed to realize that too. She moistened her lips again, and nodded her head. I opened the door, when she'd moved unsteadily aside, left it open, and crossed the hall. I knocked at George G. Gannon's door. I waited, and knocked again. I could feel my silent audience behind me . . . Viola Kersey and Molly McShane. Otherwise I don't suppose I would have had the temerity to turn Mr. George G. Gannon's doorknob. But I did. I turned it, and oddly enough the door opened, almost as if it hadn't been completely closed when I touched it.

"Mr. Gannon," I called.

There was no answer. I looked into the lighted room. He wasn't there. The bathroom and closet door, like mine, were open, the windows open onto his patio. Mr. Gannon was not at home. He'd been in deshabille, or at least I assumed so, seeing his heliotrope pajamas and holly-green dressing gown and holly-green sandals in a heap in the middle of the floor. Either he'd not been there when Mrs. Kersey left his room or he'd left it since. With the emotional crisis going on in my room, it wouldn't have been strange if we'd failed to hear him go.

I closed the door at once.

"He *was* there," Mrs. Kersey said.

"He's not there now."

She put her hand to her throat. "I can't go down there alone. I can't."

"I'll go with you," Molly said. "I'm not afraid."

She stepped forward, chin still up, contemptuous of Mrs. Kersey and contemptuous of cowardice itself.

"No, you won't," I said. "I'll call the desk, and one of the boys can go with her. You're staying here with me."

I went over to the phone and told the operator to send one of the boys down. While I did it I read the three yellow slips that were there beside it and that I hadn't noticed when I came in. They were the carbons of the originals I would have found in my box if I'd gone by the desk. The time stamped on them was ten minutes past eight for the first and eight-thirty for the last. They were all from Lucille Gannon and each marked *Urgent—Please Call*.

It was almost eleven then, but I called anyway. After I told the operator we'd like a bellboy, I asked her to ring Mrs. Gannon for me in Room 203.

"Oh, she's gone, Mrs. Latham," the girl said cheerfully. "Haven't you heard? They've taken her to the hospital. She turned on the gas heater in her bathroom and forgot to light it. She must have thought it had a pilot light. It's lucky the woman upstairs could smell. They got her out and they hope she'll be all right, but it was a narrow squeak. We've sure had a lot of excitement around here lately. Mr. Gannon's gone with her. He's terribly upset. I guess anybody would be. I'll send a boy, Mrs. Latham. Right away."

I put the phone down. It was cold and heavy as lead in my hand.

"It's Lucille," I said. "She turned on the gas and forgot to light it. She's——"

I didn't get any further. Mrs. Kersey gave a guttural gasp as if somebody had her white throat already in his hand, slowly pressing steely claws into it. She was grey and green and mottled. She staggered to the door.

"Let me out of here! Let me out of here!"

It was a hoarse, awful cry, and she pulled the door open, and staggered back for an instant, and then she ran. She didn't wait to swing into her rhythmic walk and she didn't wait for the boy to come.

"Lucille!" Her name was a sort of awed whisper on Molly's lips as she looked at me. "Not Lucille. She wouldn't forget to light the gas. It must have been . . . somebody else, Mrs. Latham."

I nodded slowly. I thought so too. It seemed cold in the room, suddenly, but somehow I was reluctant to turn on our gas.

Molly went over and looked down toward Mrs. Kersey's apartments. "She's scared, now, isn't she?" she said quietly. "She's really scared. Maybe . . . now she'll go home. Go home and stay there."

With two people dead and one near death, and Sheep's sending Molly to my room because he didn't think she was safe in her own, Mrs. Viola Kersey's being so scared that she'd go home and stay there seemed to me a shockingly small net result . . . even if she lived to get home. It frightened me. Murder I'm used to. My life with Colonel Primrose and Sergeant Buck had at least done that for me if nothing else. But before, it had always been a reasonable sort of murder. It had never been creeping and sly, so mad, so without discernible pattern. If it was all to frighten Viola Kersey away from Hollywood it was time something was done about it.

And it was certainly time for me to start taking to heart Colonel Primrose's constantly reiterated lecture on Dangerous Knowledge. There was no doubt, I supposed, that I had it. There was no doubt in that case that I'd better begin to get rid of it. What had happened to Lucille could be part of it.

I went to the telephone. "What's Eustace Sype's number, Molly?"

Her little body stiffened, storm warnings running for the approaching squall.

"What do you want it for?"

"I want to tell Colonel Primrose about Lucille Gannon," I said patiently. If I'd thrown the telephone book at her it wouldn't have surprised me. "I don't think Lucille turned the gas off either. They ought to know it up there."

She considered that a moment.

"If you truly believe your parents had nothing to do with any of this, Molly, you won't be afraid for the police to know."

I'd hit her much closer to home than I'd had any idea I would or could. It was the first inkling I'd had that her passionate defense of them came from anything deeper than a belief that they were innocent. It was a startling revelation, and profoundly disturbing. I could see her crumpling up inside, fighting down the miserable agony of doubt that she was living with in her heart.

"They couldn't have, Mrs. Latham," she whispered. "They couldn't have. Not Lucille. They haven't got anything against Lucille Gannon . . ."

I started to say something in general, and stopped. There didn't seem much use, at this point.

"Then what's the telephone number?"

She gave it to me. She didn't want to, but she did. She stood there then with her little fists knotted tightly together, her lips trembling, watching me, trying desperately to keep from breaking down altogether.

It took me a long time to get the house, and when I did I could hear the blur of heavy voices all around the telephone even when I was speaking to Colonel Primrose, telling him about Lucille.

He listened in absolute silence, and he was silent for a long time when I'd finished.

"What hospital is she at?" he asked then.

"I don't know," I said. "You can find out. But I *told* you she was afraid. George Gannon's with her. She was terrified, this afternoon. I think somebody ought to go and be with her."

"You're right," he said.

That was in itself an all-time high. But everybody's got to be right once . . . even me.

"And if you'll come in the morning, there's some other stuff I think I'd better tell you," I said.

I should have known better than to say it. It was a bad mistake, and I knew it the instant the words were out of my mouth.

Molly was watching me, every inch the little jungle cat again, poised, intense and taut, ready to spring. I mean figuratively. What she did in fact was to draw in a quick audible breath, and flash around, and the next instant she was out the door and gone. I could hear her feet on the flagstones. She was running, and I hadn't the faintest doubt where she was running to. She was heading for a telephone . . . just as she'd done when she recognized the name of Viola Van Zant Kersey, and in her frantic haste had left her bag behind her in the telephone booth, to be picked up there by the girl from Seattle.

As I turned away from my own phone, I felt suddenly and terrifyingly alone. The silence all around me was thick and soft as sable down. The long night stretched endlessly ahead of me, already filled with formless nameless moving things.

That's when I remembered the yellow match book cover on the seat of the taxicab in Washington, D. C.

"Death is the Devil's Stronghold," someone had written on it. The fear of death was really worse, I was thinking. It's the outer battlements of the fiery keep. It's the paralyzing chain that drags to the gates. I could feel it now. I could feel the creeping whispering Presence moving up the dark patio stairs, slithering across the tiled floor of the hall outside my door. I've never been so frightened in my life.

CHAPTER TWENTY-FOUR

IT WAS HALF-PAST TWO when I heard George Gannon come home.

I'd been asleep and awake a hundred times, it seemed like, and heard a hundred creeping footsteps, before I heard him. When I first went to bed I'd left the light on in the bathroom and the windows closed, but I was ashamed about the light and turned it off when the stuffiness of the room woke me the first time. I even closed the door to keep out the glow from Viola Kersey's lights, full on, before I decided to open the windows and get a little fresh air come what might. The white iron furniture on the patio had the reassuring quality of familiar objects. I don't say my liver wasn't still the pallid shade of a piece of old halibut, but at least some of the oppressive closed-in feeling of locked windows and tightly drawn curtains was removed.

It was the smell of cigar smoke coming in through the screen that first told me George Gannon was outside. That in itself was a little surprising. The impression I'd got was that he ate his cigars cold.

Smoking one hot would seem to indicate a calm and peaceful spirit. It couldn't, I thought, be that he was content with his wife's condition . . . or could it? If Lucille Gannon was right, and George Gannon was himself the heavy in this grim tale he was acting in for once—and directing, and producing as well, I supposed, if she *was* right—then the only reason he'd have for enjoying his cigar at this time of night must be that she was worse off than the girl at the switchboard had thought.

It was a sobering idea. I'd half forgotten what it was Lucille had been practically shouting at the top of her lungs when it had struck her that he might be listening. It came back to me very clearly now. I remembered chiefly her dreadful questions about evidence. Would Eustace Sype's saying he'd seen George be enough, or would they have to *prove* he'd done it? And I remembered the way Lucille, thinking suddenly that he could have heard her, had clutched her throat. That was fear, as genuine and stark as it was in the hoarse croak that Viola Kersey had let out when she heard about Lucille.

It occurred to me at just that point, I think, that the smoke from George Gannon's cigar was very close.

That was also the time I got up. I got up, put on my dressing gown and stayed up. I stayed up until George Gannon went back into his room to stay. That was at twenty minutes past four. From a quarter to three until that time, except for a short space when he answered the telephone, George Gannon paced. He didn't stay on the patio; I heard the muted click of his gate, and his awkward steps going down to the terrace. And I gathered eventually that his spirit was anything but calm and peaceful. He was a harassed and sleepless soul. It was a story told in sound as he paced back and forth, up and down. What his thoughts were I'd have liked to know. I'd have liked to go out on my own patio and call to him to ask how Lucille was, but I didn't dare do that. It was a strange trio that he and Viola Kersey and I made there in our adjacent holes . . . George Gannon pacing, me wide awake, awaiting my passport into the Devil's Stronghold, Viola Kersey enshrined in her glowing pool of light below us, waiting for hers with even more acute and agonizing fear. In the sunlit morning it was absurd. It wasn't absurd at half-past three, the silence broken only by George Gannon's slippered feet pacing, pacing, pacing.

At ten minutes past four the telephone ringing in his room took him inside. I could hear it through the open windows on the patios. He was down on the terrace walk, by the chrysanthemum bed, when it rang. He ran up the steps, clicking the gate sharply, letting the screen door bang shut behind him. I thought he'd gone to stay then, but he hadn't. He came out onto the patio again, and I heard the creak of the chaise longue as he threw himself on it.

Then I heard him sobbing. It was a soul-racking, terrible sound coming in strangled torment across the white painted brick wall that divided his patio from mine, the wall with the fuchsia on it, the blossoms crimson and purple like great drops of blood dripping down its dead white face. George Gannon was crying. Lucille was dead, then. He'd been pacing, then, waiting for the news to come, with what anxiety, and even horror, perhaps, his despair now was the vivid proof. And it was a strange thing, but I was no longer afraid. I was aware suddenly that I was no longer afraid of the creeping night things. I looked at the clock at the head of my bed. It was twenty minutes past four. I'd started to take off my dressing gown and go back to bed, when I heard the creak of his chaise longue again, and I heard the screen door open then, and shut. He'd gone back to his room, the racking torment of his weeping eased finally to give him rest. It's a horrible thing, to hear a man cry. And after I went to bed again it seemed to me I could still hear him, and I still felt pity for him.

Which, I suppose, is what made it such an appalling shock the next morning when Colonel Primrose called me and said Lucille was all right and she'd probably be out of the hospital around ten o'clock. I was utterly staggered. I wouldn't have been nearly so staggered if somebody had told me Viola Kersey had been found with a rope around her neck. And nobody told me that. My son, who brought me my breakfast in his capacity of morning waiter, told me what amounted to the contrary, in fact. Mrs. Kersey was very much alive and well. Even more, she was in high good spirits. She'd started packing, the night before; this morning she'd changed her mind. She loved it in Hollywood, she was going to stay.

I was still so confounded about the business of Lucille that Mrs. Kersey's new intentions, while interesting, were a relatively minor surprise.

"Here's your paper, Mother," Bill said. "I'm rushed now, but I'll be back. The Colonel wants us to keep still about last night."

He disappeared. He didn't want to talk about it himself. I could tell from the way he put it off on Colonel Primrose and the sleepless drawn look around his eyes. In the back of my mind I was thinking again about George Gannon weeping on the patio. That it could have been sheer heartfelt relief that Lucille was all right hadn't occurred to me, somehow. I was too conditioned to storm and stress at the moment to remember, even, that there were simple emotions. Even in Hollywood there could be simple ones. They didn't all have to be road shows in Technicolor. That was the trouble with Lucille that I'd been objecting to from the beginning. The emergency long distance calls about nothing at all, the telegrams, the Air Mail Special Delivery letters . . . especially the one that had Bill doing a nose-dive down the primrose path. I glanced at the three orange memos by my telephone. They were marked *Urgent*. It was the cry of Wolf, Wolf once too often. When she really had an urgent need, I hadn't believed her.

But all that was highly futile. I relaxed, or tried to, and opened my paper. On the front page was a signed piece by a Hollywood columnist. It said "Flash!" at the top of it, and there was a woman's picture. I looked three times before I believed it. It was an old and very coy, not to say very sappy, pose of the young Viola Van Zant, with bobbed curly hair down over one eye and her skirts above her knees, cheesecake of another day. Below it was the story.

"I promised Viola Van Zant—she's Mrs. Samuel C. Kersey now, and very happily married to more moola than you and I will ever see—that I wouldn't tell anybody she was back in Hollywood. When she called me she was all excited about a story she wants her former husband, Producer George Gannon, to do. She believes in it so much she's ready to put up the money for it, and that's believing in something, believe me. I wouldn't mention it now except that last night George Gannon's present wife, the former Mrs. Baldwin James, had a terrible accident out at the Casa del Flores. They say she forgot to turn off the gas in the bathroom heater. I for one don't believe for an instant that it was anything but an accident, and just because it happened when George's first wife was at the hotel isn't any reason for their friends jumping to any other conclusion. Mrs. Gannon is a gracious and charming woman and I hope she'll be all right very soon. It's hard on George when he's had so much trouble getting started on 'Death on the Back Stairs' which he's shooting over in the Valley. Of course I've always said it was such a pity he and Viola broke up before success came to him. When they got their divorce she was very sad about it. She said she and George loved each other very deeply, but they had decided it was better for each of them to go their own way, and I was glad when both of them found happiness. And for those people who think marriage can't be a success in Hollywood, I'd like to point out that the George Gannons have been very happily married for three years now. It would make me very unhappy to think anything was upsetting it, because just a few months ago George called me up and said, 'Mabel, I've never been so happy in my life.' I hope there hasn't been any misunderstanding between him and Lucille because Viola is a sincere, loyal, and lovely person, and we're all glad she's back with us again."

. . . Lucille Gannon had tried to commit suicide. It didn't say so, but implication could go no further. It stood up like the Tower of Babel on the plains. I looked through the paper, trying not to think about it. And it was a queer thing. If there was anything at all in that paper about Washington, D. C., or Lake Success, I didn't notice it. Normally, I'm told, people make a feeble and frustrated effort to hang on to the old world at least for a week, when they've come to this new one. They all give up sooner or later, though not usually as quickly as I'd done. It was all too vivid and exciting, the rest of the world dim and old shoe. What was happening on Capitol Hill hadn't the slightest interest to me, compared with what was happening in the Casa del Flores, or Bel Air or Hollywood, or even Los Angeles, where the police had that morning found another body under a pepper tree and another starlet had married another millionaire whose third wife was suing him to get back her jewels and fifteen hundred a week to buy the baby a new pair of shoes.

Nevertheless, I couldn't stop thinking about Lucille, try as I might —and I knew her turning on the gas and saying goodbye to it all made no sense whatever . . . not even out here, in this brave new world where people pay ninety cents for an avocado on the Sunset Strip when they have a treeful of them in their own back yard. Lucille was not the suicide type. I stopped for a moment. Or was she? Could that explain her husband's soul-racking sobs at ten minutes past four in the morning? I decided that instead of racking my brains, I'd wait and rack Colonel Primrose's.

He came at half-past nine. At nine the bellboy had brought me a telegram. It was for the Colonel. I'd almost opened it when I saw it was in care of me, not to me. He read it and put it in his pocket without comment. He was in one of those difficult moods, uncommunicative but brusque, and his usual amused and urbane detachment from the foibles and follies of less disciplined mortals was gone. He was a man with much on his mind and apparently not getting too far with getting it off.

"Lucille told the hospital people she was coming here," he said. "I want to see her as soon as she gets here, and I want to see her husband. I also want to see this Mrs. Kersey."

"What about Eustace?" I asked.

I had the awful feeling that Eustace Sype, dead, was going to be like the dead girl from Seattle, quietly shunted into the grave because Captain Crawford didn't want Viola Kersey killed.

He shrugged. "The Shavins are trying to put their heads in a noose. They don't know what was in the papers Shavin burned. They were at the house all day. Nobody could have come and gone without their knowing it, because of the dogs. Except for that, it would have been simple for anybody. It wouldn't take five minutes to come in, grab the bayonet off the wall, slit the back of the seat, puff up the cushions, insert the bayonet, see the base was firm against the lower chair frame and be on the way—except for those dogs. It would have been a noisy five minutes, and the Shavins couldn't have missed it. So, their story being true, one or both of them did it, or they knew who did. And they deny it."

"But they could have missed it very easily, as a matter of fact," I said calmly. "For the simple reason that they weren't at the house all day."

The look he gave me had a little bayonet quality itself.

"Nobody was out there to answer the phone when Lucille kept calling. Rose was right out in back here, at half-past four. I saw her. I told you I had some stuff to tell you."

He drew a deep breath. "You wouldn't like to hold it out another week or so?"

I'm sure Mrs. Kersey would have had some involved semantic

cliché ready. I wasn't fool enough to expect any gratitude, but I wasn't prepared to have my head snapped off in place of it. I remembered one is supposed to count ten when an irascible male is present.

"Go ahead. What stuff have you?"

CHAPTER TWENTY-FIVE

I TOLD HIM. I told him about Rose winding the hemp string off the stakes under the chrysanthemums and about the section of it by George Gannon's steps that was already gone, where the plants had fallen over. From there I went back and told him all I knew—about Molly's bag and what I presumed to be a letter from Mrs. Kersey, and the girl from Seattle, and about Mrs. Kersey and Eustace Sype, and the scene at his house with Rose and Morris Shavin and Molly McShane. I told him about Lucille, and about George Gannon weeping on the patio. Once started, I must have sounded as Niagara Falls would if it was dammed up and let loose again. Then I started to show him the morning paper.

"I've seen that."

He reminded me a little of George Gannon pacing up and down his patio, only Colonel Primrose confined himself to the inside of my room.

He stopped at last and stood looking at me with an oddly puzzled expression on his face.

"I can't really believe it," he said. "It's all there, in plain sight. But it's incredible. It's . . . it's incredibly stupid."

Lucille came then. She looked really awful. I could still smell the nauseating aura of gas around her . . . in her hair and the clothes she had on. She was a sort of near olive-green, the lines at the corners of her mouth etched deeper than ever. She sank down in the bamboo chair and closed her eyes.

"I don't want to talk," she whispered.

"You should have stayed in the hospital."

"I couldn't. I couldn't stand it there."

"I want to be sure you knew what you were telling me last night.

Your husband came to your room. He turned on the gas for you because it was chilly. You had a drink out of a bottle of whisky he'd brought. You went to bed as soon as he'd gone, and you don't remember anything more. You didn't touch the gas heater at any time. Is that right?"

She nodded slowly. Colonel Primrose went to the phone. "Will you ask Mr. George Gannon to come over to Mrs. Latham's room, please."

"Oh no, Colonel! I can't see him!"

"I'm not interested in Mr. Gannon's orders. I'm representing the County Sheriff. Tell him to come over here at once, please. Room 102, across the hall."

Lucille bent her head forward in her hands. "He won't like it. He was furious with me when I called him last night. He came to my room, but he hated it. And he hated me."

"What time did he come there?"

"Just before I went to bed," she said wearily. "I called Grace to ask her to come, but she wasn't in. We had a drink, and he seemed to have calmed down. I was so sleepy before he left I didn't care much what mood he was in. I just went to bed."

"And you don't know anything else about it at all?"

"No."

She let her head rest on the cushion, her eyes closed. She looked ghastly, and frightfully ill, and when we heard the door across the hall open and George Gannon coming over, she was shaking so she had to close her teeth on her lower lip to steady it.

Gee Gee had on a yellow T-shirt and emerald-green slacks. The perspiration was already blooming in ever-increasing blobs on his nearly unthatched skull. He looked at the Colonel, and at me, and at Lucille. Lucille didn't open her eyes, and she kept her face turned away from him.

"How is she?"

He asked it of Colonel Primrose.

"Not too good. She says you were in her room last night. You brought a bottle of whisky. You turned on the gas heater for her. She got sleepy and went to bed. You went away."

George Gannon nodded. "That's all correct."

"You had a drink together?"

"I had a drink." Lucille's voice was dull. "He didn't. He brought the whisky, but he said he had to work. He wouldn't take a drink."

Colonel Primrose looked at Gannon.

"That's right. I'm not drinking after dinner. I've got a new bottle of Scotch. I think she'll like it. So I take it over to her."

"Where did you get it?"

George Gannon looked surprised. "It's given to me as a present."

He added, when Colonel Primrose waited, "Mrs. Kersey gives it to me. It's out of her husband's private stock."

Colonel Primrose nodded without apparent interest. "I understand Mrs. Kersey is your former wife?"

"That's right."

"And that she's putting up her money for you to produce a story she's got. I'd like to know what her story is about."

Up to that point George Gannon had been fairly calm. This was as if Colonel Primrose had touched at one time all basic centers of his reflexes. He whipped a cigar out of his pocket, his peeled eyes popped out, he was off.

"Her money! That I don't need! That I don't want! Her story! That I got to see before I buy it. That I don't buy unless I see how much she throws in the pot. Does she bring it to me? No! She gives it to Eustace Sype—I sign, then I read. That I don't do—not if she's Fort Knox and gives me the door key. She says, they buy up Molly McShane's contract. For this story they take Molly McShane. They don't get her. I keep her. She's terrific! She's got everything! I don't sign her up for a story till that story I see!"

Colonel Primrose listened gravely.

"Did you ask Sype to let you see it?"

"Do I ask him? I am down on my knees begging him to let me see it. I go up there. I take time to go up there after Viola's lunch to say 'Let me see it, if it is any good I want to do it!' "

"What does he say?"

(I was happy to see Colonel Primrose lapsing momentarily into Mr. Gannon's jargon.)

"What does he say? He's not there! Nobody's there! No servants, nobody but those screwball dogs of his yapping their heads off out in the kitchen!"

"You know Sype is dead?"

George Gannon was suddenly quiet again. "Yes. I know it."

"You know how he was killed?"

"Yes."

"I'm told it was an idea you and he cooked up together one afternoon."

I didn't understand him, but George Gannon did. He took out his handkerchief and wiped his forehead. It needed wiping badly. He was quite pale, and for a moment he just nodded at Colonel Primrose without speaking.

"That's right," he said then. "It's an original idea we get from the Old Testament. There is a king. He is stabbed. They can't see the dagger because he's too fat. It's in his right side because a port-sider is the one who stabs him. I think if Sype will play it we can do a Biblical murder story with Arabs maybe trying to take the Holy Land. It's a dilly!"

George Gannon warmed to his story.

"This fat king's out by the marble swimming pool. The hand-maidens are staying him with flagons. This Arab slips in, grabs the bayonet off the wall in the next room, slits the silk on the back of the divan, sticks the bayonet up at an angle through the swans-down, jams the hook against the lower frame and gets out the other door. It's simple . . . an Arab boy can do it in two minutes! The fat king comes in, one hand-maiden is with him—she has a zither because this fat king likes music. He sinks down, on his cushions, and there he is! Nobody sees the bayonet. The cushion is puffed out. Nobody looks for a slit in the back. They all think he has got a stroke. By the time they get him up he is a dead duck! Nobody sees this Arab, by this time he is a mile away! It's simple murder, see? Simple murder you can tie in with a costume picture and an up-to-the-minute international slant!"

Colonel Primrose's composure was outwardly unruffled, but I thought he had some difficulty about not choking a little when he spoke next.

"Do you have to do stories about murder?"

"Do we have to do murder? Sure, we have to do murder. There are only two subjects—a woman's chastity, and murder. Nobody's interested in chastity any more. Murder's all we got left to write stories about."

I supposed that was a George Gannon original too. It seemed to me I'd heard it quoted from more gifted sources.

"I hear in the middle of the night it's the way Sype is killed.

Sheep Clarke calls me at four in the morning to tell me. He tells me he and Bill let it out when you're talking to them. I say it's okay. They got to tell what they know. I don't hold it against them."

I had the horrible fear that Colonel Primrose was going to ask him why, then, he'd stumbled out onto his patio and wept so bitterly, if that was why Sheep had told him then, and if it was all right. But instead he went back.

"That whisky," he said quietly, "has been analyzed, Gannon. It was heavily drugged."

Lucille leaned forward and put her dark head in her hands.

It wasn't a kind thing for me to do, but I couldn't help thinking just then about her two other marriages, and how merrily she'd kicked over the traces and left a pair of bewildered and pretty decent men gasping for breath with her suddenness. It would only be a kind of poetic justice, after all, if her third husband should turn out to be a different breed of cat.

After the first look he gave her, he seemed to want to forget she was there. I thought I could understand it when he next spoke—very quietly, this time, and in part at least not in his peculiar idiom.

"I realize, Colonel Primrose, I'm in an awkward situation. I believe there's nothing wrong with the Scotch when I took it there. The bottle's been opened—it's open when Viola gives it to me, because she offers me a drink, and that I don't want because I am eating too much anyway, so I bring it to my room with me. I think it's good Scotch. But I see you're collecting a lot of circumstantial evidence against me. I look at it. I say, I wonder did I do it? Am I drunk when I go out and these things happen or am I crazy?"

There was something very dignified in the way he said that, and it's hard to be dignified in a yellow open-neck shirt with short sleeves and the tail hanging out over a pair of bright green slacks. But George Gannon did have dignity then, and sincerity. I thought Lucille must feel it, as I knew Colonel Primrose did. But fear is deafening as well as blinding, and she was listening to it and not to her husband. Knowing what she believed, I couldn't blame her. And again, I realized suddenly that George Gannon hadn't actually denied he'd done any of the things the circumstantial evidence pointed to his doing. When he asked himself if he was drunk or crazy, he could answer yes to both, for all I knew.

"What do you know about Miss McShane's background, Mr. Gannon?"

It was a question that surprised me, and George Gannon opened his eyes so they looked like billiard balls with iris and pupil painted on them.

"Do you know her parents, for instance?"

"I know if she's got parents, there's something wrong with 'em."

"Wrong with them? Why?"

"Why? Because they're not trying to cash in on their daughter's contract. That, I have never heard of in all the years I am in the motion picture business. That is new. I ask Sype, where are the parents, when are they coming, wanting a lot of money, wanting a house in Bel Air, a motor car, a spot on the payroll, wanting me to pay them for taking care for their own daughter. Sype says they aren't, they are keeping out of it. That, I don't believe. I do a quick double take. I say, Sype, they're either both dead, or they are in the pen for life. Parents, aunts, brothers, sisters, cousins, half-sisters, great aunts four times removed, baby comes to Hollywood, and they're all on the lot trying to cash in. It's——"

"I think, in that case, you'd like to meet Miss McShane's parents," Colonel Primrose said. He went over to the door. I couldn't see why he was doing it, after all the agony the Shavins had gone to to keep their child's producer from finding it out. It wasn't till he'd got to the door and turned back that I had a sinking feeling he was doing it with reason.

"You've seen Eustace Sype's servants, haven't you, Mr. Gannon?"

For an instant George Gannon's eyes had the painted billiard ball effect, and his mouth dropped open a little. "Sype's *servants?*"

"Rose and Morris Shavin," Colonel Primrose said. "I believe they used to be your servants, Mr. Gannon. Rose is the night maid at this hotel. Her husband is the night watchman."

George Gannon stood there staring at him. It was as strange as anything I've seen. For one so wired for both movement and sound as he was it was doubly astonishing. He'd become quite pale again.

"I thought it might interest you."

A slow dark flush came through the pallor of Gannon's face. Lucille had raised her head from her hands and was looking at him too. I thought it was the first indication I'd had of how really profound her mistrust of him was. She saw me looking at her and turned away, her eyes fixed, staring out of the window.

"I've asked the Shavins to come here—and Mrs. Kersey," Colonel Primrose said. "I think you've been going under a . . . a set of misapprehensions too long, Mr. Gannon."

I had the feeling that I was listening to some curious lot of double-talk. The diamond bracelet, I supposed, was in some way what he was talking about. But "misapprehensions" should have included more. It didn't seem to make any kind of sense. But as Colonel Primrose had said, I had no right to set myself up as a technical expert on a commodity I had so little of.

CHAPTER TWENTY-SIX

"OH, DARLING!"

It was Mrs. Kersey who came in first, the Shavins behind her.

"Darling Lucille . . . how are you, my dear? I was horrified when I heard . . . when they told me——"

"When they told you they'd got me out alive?" Lucille was weak but caustic still.

"Darling——"

"That's enough, Mrs. Kersey," Colonel Primrose said equably. "We're all glad Lucille's alive." Or are we? I thought he might have added. But he didn't.

"Do you drive a car, Mrs. Shavin?"

Rose did a quick double take then.

"No. No, sir. I never learned to drive a car."

"Who drove you down here yesterday afternoon, when you took the cord off the chrysanthemum stakes on the back terrace here?"

In the silent room I heard the quick catch of someone's breath. Morris Shavin moistened his lips. "I drove," he said. "I drove."

"You were not at Mr. Sype's the whole day then."

Rose folded her hands in front of her. They were trembling again. "No, sir."

Colonel Primrose nodded. "It was foolish of you to say you were. Because while you were away the murderer of Eustace Sype had the opportunity to go up there and carry out the plan Sype and Mr. Gannon had figured up for their murder of a very fat man who loved a cushioned divan to sit in. It couldn't have been done if you were both in the house with the dogs to give warning that someone else was there."

"We were gone only an hour . . ."

"Ten minutes was enough," Colonel Primrose said evenly, "for a mind that had a plan and an urgent need."

Then he changed his question abruptly. "What was it your husband burned?"

Her lips compressed to an obdurate line. "I don't know. Mr. Sype told us to burn it if anything happened to him."

George Gannon had moved over to the window. He stood there watching them, his cigar smoke making a Los Angeles smog through which he could be seen but darkly. He reminded me suddenly of Molly, coiled up like a steel spring, ready to fly apart with devastating intensity.

Colonel Primrose reached into his pocket and took out the telegram he'd just got. He handed it to Rose.

"I'd like you to read that. I think you know what was in the papers you burned."

Then he turned to Mrs. Kersey. She was in a pink slack suit with pink tourmalines, this morning, instead of her blue slacks with sapphires. "I think you could also tell us, Mrs. Kersey. But I'll save you the trouble. What was burned was the script you want Mr. Gannon to produce. He's anxious to know what it's about. Will you tell us?"

Mrs. Kersey's jaw dropped. She looked over at Rose Shavin, blinking. She turned calmly back then to Colonel Primrose.

"It's stupid of me, but I've forgotten entirely," she said. "It was just a little thing I scribbled on the train coming out. I didn't even let dear George read it, I was so ashamed of it. Eustace was going to have a writer run over it before we showed it to him."

"You wanted Molly McShane to appear in it, I think?"

"I thought the sweet child was perfection for it. I truly did."

Rose was holding the telegram in her hands, her face the most extraordinary and enigmatical study. Her hands were trembling, the yellow blank in them quivering. Morry Shavin had taken her arm protectively, like a white myrtle vine steadying a shaken stone wall. Colonel Primrose took the telegram from her and put it in his pocket.

And the door burst open. Of course I'd got used to it, to Molly McShane's entrances. I could be startled, not being a mechanism with an entirely phlegmatic nervous system, but I couldn't be surprised any more. This time, however, there was a happy difference. It was not me she wanted to claw. Not for me, this time, the sulphur and the brimstone. I was no longer front man in the shooting gallery. She darted to the side of her mother and turned on us with a blazing glance that took us all in, even her producer, and finished by most particularly searing the rather surprised face of my friend Colonel Primrose, 92nd Engineers, U. S. Army, Retired, and with no Sergeant Buck to step in front of him, with granite breast bared and iron-hearted devotion.

"You! You let my father and mother alone! You haven't any right here! Let me alone, Mother . . . don't believe him. He's trying to trick you. That's what Bill says he does. Bill says——"

Then to my great relief two voices spoke as one from the doorway.

"Shut up, Molly!"

I was very glad Bill and Sheep had come on the scene in time. I'd rather Colonel Primrose didn't hear any more of the things Bill says. A beautiful friendship would have shrivelled then and there to the dust and ashes to which Morris Shavin had reduced Viola's movie script.

"Just shut up, baby . . ."

She turned on them too then, but they had authority. How they did, I didn't know, but they had it, for their burning dream boat, while the adults stood around more or less like clods. All, I should say, except one, and that was her producer. George Gannon had brightened up in spite of everything. His peeled eyes were shining. He loved it. It was as though he'd written all this himself, as soon as Molly McShane was on, and was producer and director too, and if he'd shouted "Roll 'em!" it wouldn't have surprised me in the least. All we needed was a camera man, and the dust of horses' hooves, and a face on the bar room floor, to have a good third-rate melodrama shooting right there in the exclusive precincts of Casa del Flores.

"Just keep quiet, honey," Sheep said, and the little dream boat collapsed as if a friendly torpedo had taken a whole side out of her.

Her eyes widened and looked around at us blankly, as if she'd not really seen us before through the blazing curtain of hyacinth-blue and brimstone-black.

Colonel Primrose smiled a little. "You're mistaken, Miss McShane," he said. "I have a right. I'm representing Captain Crawford, and I'm carrying out his directions."

Molly stood there between her parents, with Sheep, quiet and steady, behind her. He was wonderful. He was a balance keeping his dream on an even keel on a stormy sea. I saw her turn and look up at him. On her intense little face was the kind of faith and trust, lighted with a momentary radiance, that was really profoundly moving from such a hot-headed, wilful little wench. He smiled down at her. It was really a faint warming of his lean determined face rather than a smile, as he nodded at her, reassuring her. She bent toward him, almost imperceptibly, the way a flower bends, as if she were moving toward her own sandy-haired freckled Sun-god. And somehow he looked like one standing there behind her, because her faith and love made him one.

"There is rather more than one point to clear up, here," Colonel Primrose was saying. "For one, I think Miss McShane will be glad to have Mr. Gannon know neither of her parents is a thief. It's not vital for him to know—unless he remembers he was given to understand they stole a diamond bracelet from him and his wife . . . now Mrs. Kersey."

I thought the star of the silent screen seemed to have lost, suddenly, a little of her pink rosebud bloom.

"I don't see why we need to go into that, Colonel Primrose," she said with some asperity. "Everyone makes mistakes. I made one, and I made restitution. I paid the insurance company the money they paid for the bracelet."

George Gannon took his cigar slowly out of his mouth.

"And the reason you took the bracelet, Mrs. Kersey?" Colonel Primrose asked politely.

"I needed the money." She snapped it out at him.

"For what?"

Molly McShane shook off Sheep's protecting arm and took one step forward in front of Rose and Morris Shavin.

"For me," she said quietly . . . but I knew it wouldn't be quietly for long.

Her chin was out, her blue eyes as steady as her voice.

"She took it to pay Rose and Morry to take me and say I was their child, not hers, and take care of me, so she wouldn't be bothered, and could marry again and not have a baby trailing along with her—so nobody would even know she had a baby. That's what she took the bracelet for. And she pretended Rose and Morry had stolen it! And then, when they'd done everything in all the world for me, and been so good and kind and beautiful to me, she comes and tries to take me away from them! She never cared about me, never cared whether we starved or were sick or whether we died, until she thought I might be a star. She didn't come and try to help us until she thought I was on my way, when Sheep and Bill and Mr. Gannon and even poor Eustace Sype had helped me and got me a chance out here. And then she tries to take me back. Not for me, not because she's sorry, but because she's a chiseller, and because she thinks it might help her to make a comeback in Hollywood. And she even wrote it all in a story. Only the end was different. Eustace showed it to me. The end she wrote was where the long lost child rushes into the mother's arms, now the mother's a great star again, and because the old servants were cruel and wicked to her!"

The contempt in her voice, the blasting look she gave the full-blown rose in pink slacks, would have reduced an ordinary ego to strawberry pulp. I saw again that under her flabby exterior Mrs. Viola Kersey was made of determined stuff. She stood her ground, cool and watchful.

"But that isn't the way the story ends, Mrs. Kersey! You're not a star and Rose and Morry are not cruel and wicked! They're good and kind and wonderful and they're the only parents I've ever had! You can threaten us with the law and everything else!"

She flashed around to me. "That's what was in her letter in my bag that I didn't want you to see. She said she'd been deceived, Rose and Morry had told her I was something dreadful that had better be put away somewhere . . . and fortunately now she had money to fight for her baby child. And no court with the kind of lawyers she could afford to hire would resist a mother's prayer. A mother's prayer! And she said she was keeping all the letters I'd written her, when she first started writing to me three months ago, to show the courts how Rose and Morry had poisoned my mind against her.

"That's why I went down to her room the night I found out who she was, to find the letters so she could never use them. Rose and Morry never poisoned my mind—they only told me about her at all because they were so humble they thought I wouldn't have ambition if I thought I was their child. I wish they'd never told me! I'd rather think I was their child than hers!"

She gave Viola Kersey another searing flash.

"And then, because they're simple and . . . and unworldly, and believe what they read about the courts, and money, she blackmails them with the piece of string that girl fell over. They know they didn't put it there—she says nobody will believe them, because they were right there. If she can't have me to make a splash with she'll ruin them both. So Rose decided it was best for me to go to her. Eustace Sype talked her and Morry into it, frightened them into it, with her help. He promised not to let her use her story if I went. So I was going—long enough to keep her from hurting them. But not any longer. Not a minute longer. Because she's not my mother! Rose is my mother and Morry's my father!"

"Don't be absurd, dear."

Mrs. Viola Van Zant Kersey spoke with all the ease and aplomb in the world. She'd learned more than how to walk with rhythmic grace and where to place her honeyed tones. She even smiled, lightly.

"Don't be absurd. Morris is not your father . . . and I resent that. I never was an unfaithful wife. You may remember that George Gannon was my husband at the time . . ."

It was like a destroyer getting a twelve-inch shell direct hit. George Gannon's jaw dropped. His cigar hit the floor. He stood gaping, first at his former wife, then at the child who'd been thrust full-grown into his paralyzed arms. The child was just as stunned.

Mrs. Kersey was as bland as Colonel Primrose himself.

"I take it Rose and Morris never bothered to defend my good name. I take it they never told you about the birds and the bees . . . It so happens that nobody ever told Mr. Kersey either. He preferred to think I was young and unspoiled. I certainly couldn't afford at the time to disillusion him. Men's illusions have to be fostered or women would have a hard time getting along with them. And you'll remember a star couldn't have babies, in Hollywood in my day, though now if they don't they have to adopt them by the dozen. And of course if I had told George he was about to be a father he would have made a terrible fuss about it, and if he wanted a child it would be quite simple for him to marry again and have one. It was just very inconvenient for me, at the moment, and Rose said she'd take you."

Molly McShane and George Gannon were still gaping open-mouthed and open-eyed at each other, and Rose and Morry Shavin were making silent keening motions, and my son and Sheep had miraculously found themselves something very funny in the situation and were holding themselves in with a good deal of effort. And somewhere in all this, the first conversation I'd had with Lucille Gannon was being very vividly acted again off-stage in the wings of my memory. This was what she'd sent me to Eustace Sype to find out . . . not that Molly was Rose and Morry's daughter but that she was Viola Kersey's and George Gannon's daughter. That was the reason for all the violence and heat, and the sudden switch when she thought she'd said too much. This was why she'd been down on Molly from the beginning, and why she'd sent for me to come from Washington, and why, again, she'd tried to maneuver Sheep and Molly into marrying—to get a young and lovely stepdaughter out of her way. She'd said Eustace told her hoping she'd tell her husband, and that Gee Gee would no doubt rush out and buy another diamond bracelet to atone for the parents' sins. As I saw it now, she'd stopped herself each time she realized her anger and jealous torment were leading her down a path that she couldn't afford to travel.

"—So now you see, dear," Mrs. Kersey said—and this was the beginning, I can see it now, of the end that would have been so incredible in the pedestrian world most of us live in—"it all works out beautifully. Life *is* Beautiful, if we look at it the Right Way. Dear Eustace Sype saw it all, so clearly. He said what we should do, darling, now that you've inherited my ability as an actress, is for me to come back, for me and George to marry again, and give you the sort of thing you need. With my money to allow George to really put you over, it's Ideal. I'll be glad to buy Rose and Morris a little farm somewhere. We'll need smarter-looking servants in the house. I've already seen a lawyer about Mr. Kersey. And I'm sure dear George wouldn't want you to have a stepmother, charming as Lucille is . . ."

CHAPTER TWENTY-SEVEN

I THINK that was the first time any of them had thought about Lucille. It was certainly the first time I'd dared to look at her. And then, when I did, I saw that Colonel Primrose's steady gaze, grave and somber and intent, was already fixed on her, and I had the sudden feeling that he had been watching her for some time. After all, she was too sick a woman to take this. I realized that this was Hollywood. But having a stepdaughter you were already violently jealous of suddenly rung in on you was bad enough anywhere, without also having her mother decide quite pleasantly to push you into the marital garbage can without a please, madam, or a by your leave. If there was something just incredibly absurd about the whole thing, Lucille had never had any sense of humor to speak of.

She certainly had none now. As I followed Colonel Primrose's level glance I saw she was sitting bolt-upright, the lines on her face not etched but dug with chisel and eaten with acid. To make everything worse if possible, the solid figure of Captain Crawford was in the patio door. When he'd arrived, I had no idea. He looked as if he'd been there some time. And he too was looking at Lucille as she sat gripping the cushion of the bamboo chair. Her scarlet-tipped fingers seemed to have drawn live blood out of her tortured insides, and the expression on her face chilled my heart.

"Don't look at me—what are you all looking at me for?" she said hoarsely. "Let her marry him. I don't care if she marries him. Let her take him. I don't want him. Let him get her money the way she's got Mr. Kersey's and she'll see. She's a fool. I knew they were trying to do this. But he'll get rid of her . . . the way he tried to get rid of me last night."

George Gannon took a step toward her, his hands raised in a gesture of helpless protest. He could as well have tried to stop a rushing mad river of burning gasoline let loose down the side of the canyon we were in.

"I knew you'd planned it that way. Eustace Sype put you up to it. He hated me and he was trying to make you get rid of me. That's

157

why he got Bill and Sheep to palm off your daughter on me, so when Mrs. Kersey came back there'd be two of them against one of me. But it didn't work. I wouldn't take her. Then Eustace told you to come here and send me to Palm Springs . . . so you'd be alone with her. You lied to me. You said you didn't know she was here. All the time you were waiting for her to come to you. To—"

"—And you came to the hotel too, Lucille?" Colonel Primrose's voice was quiet as ever, and like iron. "You were the woman on Mr. Gannon's patio, Wednesday night? And when you saw Mrs. Kersey come in, you couldn't take it—and you got that cord from the chrysanthemums and tied it at the top of her steps?"

"I was in Palm Springs, Wednesday night, Colonel Primrose . . . where he'd sent me to be out of his way . . . out of their way."

"I believe not, Lucille. Your husband is a great gentleman. He's lied throughout to shield you—even when it's been apparent you've been trying desperately to incriminate him. Even when you've killed two people and put on a fake attack on yourself in such a way that all three of them would point to him at once."

He turned to George Gannon.

"It's in the record, Mr. Gannon. Why you lie to defend a woman who's trying to put the noose around your neck I don't know. You told Captain Crawford at first that you hadn't seen any woman that night. When you realized Mrs. Kersey was saying there was a woman on your patio, and you heard about that girl wandering around, you changed your story. You said it was the girl who'd come to your patio. That was false. She never came there. The woman who came there was your wife . . . while Eustace Sype was there, at first, enjoying driving a woman to despair . . ."

"It's a lie! It's a horrible lie! If he told you I was there it's because he didn't succeed in killing me last night!"

"He didn't say you were there, Lucille. You told Mrs. Latham that the business of the string on the steps was out of a picture your husband's making. You're trying to accuse him because you failed to kill Mrs. Kersey, which you tried to do when you saw her in your husband's room. Let me tell you what you thought and did. You thought Mrs. Kersey would tell him Molly was her daughter and his, ask him to divorce you and take up their lives again. You knew Eustace Sype had proposed the divorce. You've divorced two husbands already when you thought you'd better yourself. You couldn't believe the third wouldn't do the same to you. You were jealous of the girl who was his daughter. You hated her, and you hated the mother more because she had money you thought your husband would sell himself and you and everything for. You didn't stop to think he might be a gentleman, Lucille. You weren't worth the despair he felt when he knew, finally, last night that you'd killed Eustace Sype, and you were making that too look as if he'd done it, again using a gag technique he'd worked out . . . and when he realized you were trying to make it look as if he'd attempted your life when it was you who'd faked it—the gas turned on again, after he'd gone leaving his fingerprints there, turned on again just a little, in a room in a hotel crowded with people——"

"That's all a lie!" Lucille cried. "All a lie! You're trying to trick me and you can't do it! I was in Palm Springs Wednesday night——"

"I'm not trying to trick you and you weren't in Palm Springs. You drove there after you'd put that cord across the steps. You got there early Thursday morning in time to answer that police call and to come back by the plane. You got here, and the first thing you did was tell Mrs. Latham, virtually, that your husband had killed the girl. You knew Gannon knew you were here, and you knew Sype knew it. That's why you killed Sype—using your husband's own gag technique again, telling Mrs. Latham you were frantic because you thought Sype might be with the police when nobody answered the phone at his house. And you were frantic— so frantic that you rushed to his house and prepared his death with the bayonet. You didn't even need any mechanical ingenuity you have to do it. It was a simple domestic matter, given the framework of a seat, great cushions of puffed down and the bayonet in the next room. It didn't take you long, Lucille—but time was of the essence and you couldn't stop to change your tire when it went flat on your way back to the hotel. With Sype out of the way and your story of coming from your own empty house with your overnight bag you thought you'd be safe. It would just be your husband's word against yours. But you made a terrible mistake, Lucille . . . you didn't realize that you were seen, here in the patio, Wednesday night, by still another person."

Lucille Gannon's eyes, slow, hunted, moved dreadfully around the room.

"That's in the transcript too. Morris Shavin, Wednesday night, was hunting for the girl. In his statement to Captain Crawford he said he almost mistook another woman for her. He would have stopped her, and got into trouble, if she had not gone out the end gate and got into her car just in time. He'd almost lost his job once by stopping a lady star he'd failed to recognize when she was visiting her husband. The job of night watchman, in a hotel like this, would 'drive the saints crazy.' That's why it was easy to overlook, here, one simple thing: Mr. Shavin nowhere said, in his transcript, that he didn't recognize this woman Wednesday night. The implication is that if he had stopped this woman he would again have got into a lot of trouble . . . and the reason he knew that he would is that he did recognize her. That is more than an implication; it is a fact. He did not stop her, and he has not yet told the truth, because there could be more than his own job at stake this time. Is that right, Mr. Shavin?"

The little man tried to find words, the sweat standing on his brow. It was a spot that all the citizenship papers in the world could not help him out of. He looked appealingly at Molly, at Rose, at George Gannon.

"His own job was at stake when he stopped the star," Colonel Primrose said quietly. "This time it was Miss McShane's job too. Because the woman he saw Wednesday night, going out of the grounds and getting in her car, was the wife of Miss McShane's producer and director. Is this the truth, Mr. Shavin?"

Morris Shavin found broken words. "She was going way," he said. "She not see me. She has bad temper, Mrs. Gannon. I would have stop her until I see she is the mister's wife. It was when I come back from going to his car with Mister Sype."

Lucille Gannon's eyes stared unseeingly ahead of her.

"And there is still more," Colonel Primrose said. "In the transcript again. George Gannon admits a woman was there, and says it was the drunken girl. Mrs. Kersey remarks, 'I wouldn't have told a soul, Georgie dear. I have a clean mind. I assumed it was your wife, darling.' I think perhaps——"

Viola Kersey brought her hand suddenly up to her mouth. Her face turned pale under her pink healthy makeup. She found her voice too.

"I remember. It *was* his wife. My God, he *said* it was his wife!"

She looked at George Gannon, standing silent there.

"I remember now. He *said* it was. I just didn't believe him. I . . . I thought he was lying. I thought it was a babe he had there while his wife was away. I thought he was lying because I'd surprised him, going in without waiting for him to open the door."

Lucille Gannon came to her feet, her eyes blazing . . . and when she turned savagely on Mrs. Kersey her face was hideous with envy and jealousy and hatred. It was the face of a woman whose heart was a cancerous growth . . . a woman ready to destroy herself if she could destroy her husband and the woman she thought he wanted to put in her place. Why it should have been this that she broke under I do not know. Colonel Primrose had known it would be. Viola Kersey's simple assumption, that her husband would naturally have another woman there while she was away, she couldn't take. It was the spark that set the last straw on fire, it was the root and branch, the flowers and dark fruit of the fear she'd always lived with. Captain Crawford stepped in to her side, and as she moved violently toward Mrs. Kersey he caught her two arms.

"I wish I had killed you! I tried to kill you! And you!"

She jerked around toward George Gannon. "I wish I'd turned the gas full on! They'd have got you then, your fingerprints *were* there! I'd have been glad to die!"

I closed my eyes as Captain Crawford led her out.

I didn't want to look at anyone, for the moment, in that room. Anyone, that is, except one person. Mrs. Viola Kersey I didn't mind looking at. Mrs. Kersey, too, was an almost invincible devil in her own right. She looked around the room, took a deep breath, and spoke—no one else at the moment seeming to want to.

"It certainly clears the atmosphere," Mrs. Kersey said, and she returned briskly to old business. "Now I think we can come to a proper understanding, George. I'm sure we can arrange it so the publicity won't hurt us, or Molly——"

Colonel Primrose said hastily, "Be quiet, Miss McShane!"

He turned to Mrs. Kersey. She wilted a little under his level gaze before he even spoke.

"You told Mrs. Latham that Molly McShane's mother was a wicked woman. I want to have the pleasure of adding that she's a pompous, feather-brained fool. I'm very happy to tell you that you have no moral right to the child you deserted, and you have no legal right to her. You let Mrs. Latham understand you didn't have a child. You're right. You have none. You weren't as much of a fool then as you are now. You wanted to get rid of your baby, and you did it well."

He took the telegram he'd shown Rose Shavin out of his pocket.

"This is from my associate. He flew down to Galveston last night. It was of course obvious from the beginning that the only hold you could have over the Shavins would be through the one thing they had that meant anything to them. It was obvious that at their time of life it's unlikely they'd have an only child as young as Miss McShane. Let me read you my associate's report, Mrs. Kersey. 'Baby registered Doreen Shavin, daughter Morris and Rose Shavin. Midwife died 1936. Ignore third party claim.' There's no record that that baby ever belonged to you. There isn't a court in the land that would hand her over to you now against her will. Even if you could establish parentage, there's no court in the land that would hand this girl over, after seventeen years of desertion, to a woman of bad character.

"Don't interrupt me. If Captain Crawford chooses to bring it up, you'll find there are courts that regard an accessory after the fact of murder as a very serious offender. Not to mention the offense of removing evidence from the scene of a crime . . . not to mention attempting to use it as blackmail against innocent persons."

Mrs. Kersey's rosebud mouth had sagged open. It must have been one of the few times in her life when she had nothing to say. Her face was mottled in streaks and blotches, and it was slowly turning greenish-grey.

"Sype told Mrs. Latham you planned to become duenna for a promising starlet, now that Hollywood is domesticated and respectable . . . by taking back a child you'd deserted, whom you didn't offer to help until you felt her success was assured. It hasn't worked out, Mrs. Kersey. I should greatly doubt that Mr. Gannon wants to marry you again—"

"Marry that . . . !"

George Gannon was galvanized to instant life, and what he called his former wife, while no doubt true, was not the kind of language he should have used in front of a teen-age daughter.

"And one thing more," Colonel Primrose said, affably. "I doubt if Mr. Kersey is going to be happy at the idea that you've already started divorce proceedings against him. That can also come on the record."

Mrs. Kersey was not mottled grey-green any longer. Her face was suddenly quite white.

"Let me out of here!" she gasped. "Let me out!"

No one was wanting to stop her, and I heard no regrets expressed when she'd gone, except, oddly enough, from little Miss Molly McShane.

"I feel sort of sorry for her . . . I guess she's . . ."

Her voice trailed off. Pity and compassion were elements I'd thought had been left out of the brew of fire and brimstone, but it seemed they were really there. She looked up at Sheep. She turned back to Colonel Primrose.

"Don't punish her because of me. It doesn't matter to me. I . . . I wouldn't want even to take a chance of being anything like her when I'm her age. I . . . I'm going to marry Sheep. I'm not going to try to be a star."

"Not if you're my daughter you're not!" The mere mention of motion pictures was apparently enough to hurtle George Gannon out of the domestic maelstrom two of his wives had hurtled him into. "No daughter of mine is doing slave labor in this outdoor Buchenwald. This I won't take. This——"

"This you can skip!" Miss Molly McShane said. "I'm not your daughter. I'm Rose and Morry's. That you can take, and that you can like!"

"Shut up, baby." Sheep put his arm around her and drew her to him. "I don't think Rose and Morry want us to be rude to him. He's still your original producer, baby."

George Gannon jerked his cigar out of his mouth. He grinned a little. He thrust his hand out to Sheep.

"That, I like," he said. "Take her. She's yours. We're having the biggest wedding in . . ."

He stopped, looking at Rose and Morris Shavin. I looked at them too. All the years they'd worked to get their girl here . . . and now she was on her way. They both had tears in their eyes. But they were a different kind of tears.

Rose Shavin nodded. "It's best for our girl. She needs a man who can make her behave herself. That Sheep . . ."

It's as far as she got. And nobody has to believe this. I don't believe it myself, who saw it, who was there when it happened. I still don't believe it, in spite of the fact that last week, in Washington, D.C., Colonel Primrose called me up and told me they were in town and took me to see them. I'll never believe it . . . or I'll believe, always, anything anybody tells me about Hollywood hereafter.

George Gannon had his cigar poised in mid-air, staring at Rose and Morris Shavin, their faces lighted with pride and tenderness for their little former hellcat. "That Sheep . . ." Rose said. And George Gannon bounded forward.

"This, I can't believe!"

He jammed his cigar into his mouth and jerked it out again.

"This is incredible! This is terrific! This . . . Turn around, Rose. Both of you, turn around! This, I am waiting for! All my life, for the last four months, this I am waiting for!"

He stopped, speechless for an instant with the wonder of it.

"This I am four months on my knees praying for! Rose, Morry, look! Look, Rose! Look, Morry! Five hundred a week. Not a cent more. A thousand a week. It's a story I am buying and putting on ice for four months because I am never finding two people I am seeing in it. It's wonderful! It's terrific! It's *The Birth of a Nation*, it's *The Yearling*, it's *Duel in the Sun*, it's *great!* With you, it is the Academy Award and grosses nine million! Look, Rose. Look, Morry. Molly I am not wanting. Girls like Molly, with them I am lousy. But character, that I scratch for . . . that, I will buy. Who's your agent? Call my secretary!"

It sounds absurd, that I know, but there it was. Molly and Sheep and Bill stood with their mouths and eyes open wide. It seemed impossible that George Gannon, ten minutes before hag-ridden by what the girl from Seattle could have called a couple of screwy dames and been so terribly right, had forgotten all about them. But it's a thing about Hollywood. It's the unbelievable single-mindedness of the people who make the movies, the people who do the real work that no one ever hears about. It's the air they breathe, it's the blood that keeps their hearts pumping. Their own throats they cut, and anybody else's, to make a great picture. Whatever they do, whatever they say, they believe it is the most important thing in the universe. That, they believe . . . that, they work at. It's a cockeyed priesthood, but it's a working one.

And George Gannon was working. He was like the dreary lop-eared old horses that become fiery steeds the instant they hear "Camera!"

"Somebody call my secretary!"

He had them across the hall, a couple of bewildered characters, their new proprietors right behind them. Sheep, and Molly, and my son Bill. He'd forgotten he had a mother present. And she'd forgotten for some time that she had a neighbor, until at that moment Mrs. Ansell's closet door opened and a paroxysm of coughing came through the wall.

"It's this damned climate," Mrs. Ansell said. "I'll put a stick of wood on the fire. I wish to God I could see Miss Turner, so I could go back home. They say next week . . . maybe." The closet door closed, a piece of wood rolled down on the floor. My son Bill came whipping back. He'd remembered about me just as he was bringing up the rear at George Gannon's door.

"Gee, Ma!" You'd have thought he, personally, had been tapped for the Poor Man's Clark Gable. He gave me a bear hug and a kiss. He let me go, and turned to Colonel Primrose.

"Gee, Colonel! You were swell! You did a job—I guess I've had you wrong! Thanks a million!"

He put his hand out. Colonel Primrose shook it. Colonel Primrose turned to me.

"That, I like," he said.

THE END

www.ingramcontent.com/pod-product-compliance
Lightning Source LLC
Chambersburg PA
CBHW020644180626
46816CB00003B/1112